BASTION TRILOGY

Three bastions

Three unforgettable stories

A.K. LAKELETT

Faukon Abbey Publishing

Authors note:

**Please note, this book follows British English spelling, grammar, and
punctuation.**

Ebook ISBN: 978-1-945479-19-9
Hardcover ISBN: 978-1-945479-20-5

Also by A.K. Lakelett:

Faukon Abbey Mysteries:
Remember Me?
Missing Alibi
Death of a Well-Travelled Man
Faukon Abbey Mysteries Box Set – Books 1-3
Faukon Abbey Mysteries Companion

The Good Riddance Project – Occupational Hazards Novella

Three novellas. One fortress city.
The *Bastion Trilogy* brings Valletta to life in times of war
and upheaval.
From blackout streets under siege, to modern battles over
secrets and sovereignty, to young love tested by curfew
and betrayal — these stories explore courage, sacrifice, and
defiance where stone meets sea.

Contents

BASTION OF SHADOWS

One night under siege.
One impossible choice.

A.K. LAKELETT

Faukon Abbey Publishing

Contents

BASTION
OF
SHADOWS

ONE NIGHT UNDER SIEGE.
ONE IMPOSSIBLE CHOICE

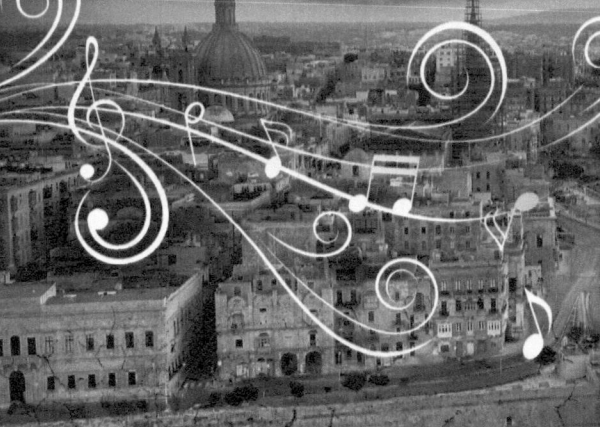

BOOK 1 IN BASTION TRILOGY
A.K. LAKELETT

Gathering storm

St Anton Gardens, mid-August, 1941

The August heat and humidity pressed on Malta like a barely wrung-out towel. Even at dusk, the air in Attard is heavy, sweet with the scent of citrus and dust. The St Anton Gardens are officially closed — but the gates had been opened for this meeting, and a pair of Home Guard men stood watch at the entrance, rifles at the ready.

Inside, the gardens had been sandbagged and shuttered, statues and fountains boarded to protect them from falling bombs. The governor's residence loomed behind blackout curtains, its windows dark.

In a small bunker room just beyond the main path, four men sit around a scarred wooden table beneath a shaded lamp.

Captain Howard Richards of the King's Own Malta Regiment leans forward, sleeves rolled up, forearms dusty.

The war has carved lines into his face that never went away, even when he smiles — which was rare.

Across from him sits Mario Cavardossi, shirt collar open, hair still smelling faintly of linseed oil. He had been working on the Madonna at St Paul's all day, high on a scaffold, painting layer over layer of blue until her robes glowed, even in the gloom of the nave. His contract to work on the statues for the upcoming *festas* for *Maria Bambina* grants him passes that allow him to travel among the villages — the perfect cover for a courier.

Next to him sits Cesare Angelotti, shoulders tense, his fingers drumming the table.

The fourth man, a civilian in a neat suit, with dust on his shoes, struck a match and lit a cigarette. He was known only as Mr Collins — a liaison from British intelligence.

"Mussolini's supply lines are moving through Palermo in greater volume," Collins says quietly, the smoke wreathing around his words. "We know they're preparing something — perhaps a push to break the convoys completely. If they succeed, Malta is done for."

Captain Richards nods grimly. "Rations are already less than half what they should be. The dockers are skin and bone."

"That's why we need good information," Collins says. He turns to Angelotti. "You said you still have contacts?"

Angelotti nods. "Dockworkers, clerks, even a few men near the airfields. They will get me manifests, troop schedules — anything that tells us what's coming before it arrives."

Collins turns to Cavardossi, "and you can move this information?"

Mario nods. "Preparing for the *festas* allows me to travel without question. I can hide papers inside stretcher frames, behind canvas rolls. No one looks twice at a man with paint-stained hands. And I meet with people in the churches."

Collins gave a thin smile. "Good. But Scarpia is watching."

The name makes Richards grimace.

"Baron Vitale Scarpia," he says. "Head of the Maltese Military Police. On paper, loyal to the Crown. Off the record — we believe he's feeding information to Mussolini's people. Nothing we can prove yet; but treat him as dangerous."

Angelotti's jaw tightens. "He had me detained last month. Next time, I may not walk out."

"Then keep your head down," Richards says.

Collins stubs out his cigarette. "Gentlemen, you know what to do. And be careful. If Scarpia catches even a hint of this network, none of you will live to see him in the dock."

They file out one by one into the warm night. The deep toll of curfew bells rolls through the air — the nightly warning before the streets go dark. Within minutes, shutters slam shut and lanterns are doused. The men melt away into the blacked-out streets, each heading for shelter.

Somewhere beyond the gardens, an air-raid siren begins to moan.

The following night – Gozo and Sicily

Angelotti's chance came quickly. At night, under a moon-less sky, he boards a weather-beaten *luzzu* at Mġarr har-bour, lying flat on the deck as the two fishermen row out past the headland.

"Keep your head down," the man mutters, "if the patrol boats catch us, we drown or hang."

Angelotti stays still as the little boat skims the water toward Sicily. Hours pass in spray and darkness, the smell of tar and salt in his nostrils.

Near dawn, they reach a small Sicilian port. Angelotti meets his contacts in a shuttered tavern, Sicilian patriots with gaunt faces and quick eyes. They pass him a packet of papers tied with twine.

"Everything we could gather," one says. "Convoy manifests, troop movements, flight schedules. Get them across the water — Malta must know."

Angelotti hides the bundle under his shirt and, before nightfall, boards another *luzzu* for the return trip. The crossing back was rougher; he arrives in Malta wet, hungry, and exhausted — but alive.

The Arrest

Angelotti barely has time to breathe before Scarpia's men, the feared Military Police takes him.

He had just crossed the square in Floriana when boots thunder from three streets at once, rifles glinting in the late afternoon sun.

He fights — Angelotti always fights — but three men brought him down. They drag him to the holding cells near the Floriana barracks, where he manages to shove the paper bundle into the hands of a carpenter pushing a cart filled with scrap wood he passes as they near the gate.

"Hide these," Angelotti gasps.

The carpenter nods and slides the packet under the wood scraps before anyone notices.

In the cell, Angelotti is left on a stone floor, beaten once, mocked by guards, half-starved.

Scarpia came by at night, looking in with a smile that makes Angelotti's stomach twist.

"Tomorrow," Scarpia says softly, "tomorrow we talk properly. Names, places, British contacts — all of it."

Angelotti spits at his boots. Scarpia laughs and walks away.

The Escape

On the second night, the guards get drunk. Their laughter echoes through the corridor, slurred singing breaking the silence.

Angelotti waits until their snores fill the hall before creeping to the door. The keys were still hanging on a nail nearby, just within reach if he stretches far enough.

It takes him nearly an hour using a twig until he finally gets the keys, praying the guards wouldn't wake and the twig wouldn't break. Finally free, he closes the cell door quietly behind him. He slithers along the wall and slips out into the narrow alley behind the barracks, his heart pounding as though it would wake the whole of Floriana.

Before sunrise, he is back at the carpenter's shop, re-trieving the hidden bundle, hiding in the shadows while heading for St Paul's Shipwreck, the one place he is sure Cavardossi would be.

Shadows in the Nave

The Church of St Paul's Shipwreck

T he city wakes like a bruised fighter: slowly, stubbornly. Valletta's August light falls hard on shattered cornices and soot-streaked limestone, showing every crack, playing with shadows on piles of rubble. Women sweep plaster dust from thresholds while anxiously looking at the sky. A cart rattles past with jute sacks and dented tins. Farther up the street, a British patrol clatters by, boots loud, tin mugs hanging from belts, a terrier trotting after them. The air smells of salt and lime and last night's smoke, layered with that chalky scent of pulverised stone that clings to a besieged city.

Inside the Church of St Paul's Shipwreck, the heat relents. The nave is a cool cave of hushed marble, the air faintly sweet with candle wax and yesterday's incense. Sunlight enters in long stripes from high windows, finding the drifting dust and the gold leaf on a side altar. The morning bells have ceased; a single fly bumbles against a pane and gives up.

Mario Cavardossi stands high on a ladder before a monumental canvas fixed to the north wall. He paints as if the brush is a vein from his heart: fast, sure, unafraid of the white spaces. The Madonna's face rises from the ground of pale plaster, strokes of warm ochre and bone black giving her the solemn fire of a woman who knows grief and faith in equal measure. It is Tosca's face—he can't help it. The curve of her cheek, the intelligence in the gaze, the mouth that can set a theatre trembling. He's been up since dawn, and the heat has pasted hair to his forehead; his shirt is streaked with pigment; his trousers are powdered with chalk.

He leans back on the ladder to judge the balance of light across the brow. Somewhere outside, a donkey brays with affronted dignity. Inside, only the faint rasp of bristles, the tiny clink when he drops a brush against the tin of turpentine.

The church door creaks. It's a commonplace sound, but Mario's hand pauses midair; nerves live shallow under skin during a siege. He turns, brush poised.

A figure edges inside and eases the heavy door shut with the care of a thief. The man is gaunt, clothes torn, hair matted with dust, one wrist banded raw where iron has bitten it. Angelotti. A gentleman reduced to bone and alertness.

"Mario," he rasps, the word catching like a cough.

Cavardossi is down the ladder in three steps. "Madonna! Cesare, they said you were taken in Floriana!"

"They spoke true," Angelotti whispers, dropping onto the nearest pew. "But last night the guards were drunk on wine, songs and self-love. When their laughter peaked, I managed to get the keys and slide the bolt." He holds up his wrist with its inflamed groove. "I ran through Floriana, keeping to the shadows when the searchlights swept the bastions. Twice I lay behind a pile of rubble while a patrol went by. A dog sniffed me and lost interest. But Scarpia—Scarpia will not lose interest. He will pry apart Malta rock by rock."

"Then you can't stay here," Mario says. "That crook and his goons search churches too." He glances up the nave toward the confessional and the sacristy door.

Angelotti drags a packet from inside his jacket—thin, creased papers wrapped with string, blotched by sweat. "These." He thrusts them at Mario. "Maps, manifests, code names, schedules of the smuggling boats. They must reach the British command tonight. If Scarpia gets them—."

Mario shoves the packet under his shirt, the paper cold and stiff against his belly. "He won't; I'll find a way. Tosca can help."

Angelotti nodded, exhausted. "God bless her."

A soft cough comes from the side aisle. Father Salvu, the sacristan—old as dust, dry as a reed—has been watching. His cassock is mended at the elbows; his ink-stained fingers give him away as the keeper of registers and notices.

"They are coming," he says in a voice not meant to carry. "You should not be here. I heard Scarpia's jackals are combing Valletta, street by street."

The sacristan looks at Cavardossi. "They were on Strada Reale not ten minutes ago. Searching houses, questioning everyone."

Angelotti stiffens like a hare hearing a snare tighten.

Angelotti catches Cavardossi's arm. "I must hide. If they find me here—"

"Family crypt," Mario says quickly. "Under the altar. Help me."

The priest is already moving, nimble with urgency for mercy's sake. Between the three of them, a narrow slab is prised aside; damp air rises, earthy and old. Angelotti swings his legs into the dark like a diver testing water.

"And the papers?" he asks, half in the grave, face chalked by the light.

"I'll get them out," Mario says. "Trust me."

Angelotti nods once and is gone. The slab slides back in place with a soft, final sound. Mario wipes lime dust on his shirt, smearing paint into new colours.

The priest makes a small, savage sign of the cross. "God forgive me disturbing the dead," he mutters, "but Scarpia and his goons are worse than damnation." Then he vanishes toward the sacristy like smoke in a draft.

The door groans again.

Floria Tosca enters like a beam of honest sunlight. Lifelong habit leads her: she pauses, dips her fingers in the stoup, touches brow, breast, left, right—an unconscious grace—before crossing the threshold of shadow. She's wearing a pale-yellow summer dress, simple, carefully mended in a discreet place only a lover would notice; the black veil of lace covering her hair makes her eyes look darker still. A wicker basket hangs from her arm—two sandwiches wrapped in paper, a small flask in a cloth, a sprig of bay tucked under the handle to keep off flies.

"Mario," she calls softly. Even the way she says his name betrays her longing. "You will make yourself ill if you go all day without eating."

He grins, the strain melting for a moment. "You are an angel," he says, "I am indeed hungry." He bends and kisses her cheek. "I'm too dirty to come closer."

She tilts her face up toward the enormous Madonna. "You have made her more beautiful," she says, and for a heartbeat there is only pride in her voice. Then the pride flickers, and jealousy's thin edge shows. "More like the Marchesa Attard, no?"

Mario flinches, just to the smallest degree. Enough for her to see. "No. It is you. Always you."

"She stood three pews from me at Mass yesterday," Tosca says, not letting him off. "Her hands. Her brow. Mario—do not make me blind for love."

"In war we see ghosts," he answers, climbing two rungs to reach a near-dry brush he needs, coming back down so he isn't speaking from on high. "If she resembles you, then the fault is mine. I have no eyes for the Marchesa or anyone else. Only for you." He reaches to tap the corner of the painted mouth with the rag; the gesture is a caress to both women at once.

She softens because she wants to, not because he earns it. But her eyes still flick to the side chapels, the confessional, the sacristy door ajar, as if the church itself is listening.

"I heard a step," she says suddenly. "Just now."

"A rat," Mario lies with the smoothness of someone who has practiced saving lives with small deceptions. "They like the wax droppings."

She looks at him for a long beat, then, faithful as breathing, reaches for the basket. "You will eat," she insists, finding the sandwiches. "Even saints must eat."

He catches her hand gently, and within that motion slips the packet from his shirt into her palm. The papers are heavier than food.

"Tosca," he says, urgency tightening his voice. "Put this under the cloth, now, please. Listen: after your concert tonight at the Manoel, you go out by the stage door. A nun will be waiting in the shadows. Give her the basket. Say nothing. Leave at once."

Her eyes jump from his to the packet. "Mario—what is this?"

"Hope," he says simply, and sees how fast she weighs words like that. Outside, a cartwheel squeals like a violin tested too far.

She slips the paper bundle under the cloth. Before she can shape a reply, the door opens with authority enough to be a blow.

Two Maltese Military Police stride in, boots ringing, rifles slung for menace and not necessity.

"Captain Scarpia requires cooperation," one announces to the altar as much as to any person. "A dangerous prisoner has escaped."

Mario moves without seeming to, placing himself so that Tosca's basket is out of direct eyeline. He straightens his back, light, but ready.

And then Scarpia himself: a black note in a slow hymn. Broad-shouldered, perfect boots, belt polished enough to catch a window's thin light. His face would be handsome if the mouth had ever learned mercy. His gloves are tucked under his arm; the smell of leather and tobacco precedes him like a calling card.

"Ah, Cavardossi," he says, polite as a snake. "And *Signorina* Tosca. What a fortune to find art and devotion in one place."

"We were at prayer," Mario says evenly.

Scarpia lifts his chin toward the wall piece. "A fine work. When it is finished, perhaps it will guard the faithful." His eyes move to Mario and rest there. "Pity the real Madonna cannot shield us from traitors."

"Angelotti is no traitor," Tosca says, too quick. She feels Mario's pulse through the air—his warning—too late.

"So," Scarpia purrs, "you know him."

"Everyone knows him," Mario says mildly. "Malta is small. Gossip is a plague you've not yet rationed."

Scarpia smiles without showing teeth. "Small islands keep small secrets poorly." He turns his head fractionally, "search."

The soldiers' boots thud along the nave. A rifle stock raps a panel, and a puff of dust rises from a saint's carved robe. One man kneels to peer under pews; another draws back altar cloths with disrespect that is the point. The sound of metal knocking stone turns the holy place into a drum.

Tosca's fingers whiten on the basket handle; the reed creaks.

From the side aisle, the sacristan passes with a broom and the thin, ferocious dignity of a man who has already decided which sins he will confess and which he will die defending. He nods to Scarpia—barely—and to Tosca with genuine warmth. In passing, he murmurs, just for her: "Your singing *Ave Maria* at the hospital yesterday was balm, *signorina*. Even the colonel tried not to weep." His eyes flick at Scarpia's men and away. "Pray."

The search turns up nothing but the echo of its own clatter. The men return, shaking their heads. "No sign, Captain."

Scarpia accepts this with the indulgence of a cat sure the mouse has only shifted to another cushion. "Then he will be found elsewhere." His gaze settles on Mario, then Tosca, then—lightly, like a finger checking the pain of a bruise—on the basket. "And when he is, I will know who fattened him for courage."

He gives a small bow, the perfect counterfeit of civility, and leaves, his men in his shadow. The door swings closed, and the church exhales.

Tosca sags onto a pew. "If they had lifted that cloth—"

"They didn't," Mario answers. "It's not bravado; they do as they're told. Tonight. The stage door. Remember." He takes her hand, it feels like holding a frightened little bird.

Father Salvu returns with a single guttering candle cupped in his hand. He traces a cross in the air toward them. "The devil himself walked through this church," he murmurs, voice rough with faith and fear. "Pray hard, my children. You will need heaven's help before this is over." He pinches the flame flat, and the wick smokes a thin thread upward.

Tosca stands and squares her shoulders the way she does before the curtain lifts. "I will sing," she says to Mario, "as if the island depends on it." He believes her; sometimes it seems it does.

They part at the door with a look that holds more conversation than speech can carry. Outside the light is harsher; a patrol shouts; a child laughs because a pigeon hops.

Teatru Manoel, later that evening

Blackout rules the city; even lanterns must be hooded. The Manoel glows like a kept secret, candlelight cupped by gilt and velvet. The Manoel is packed despite the siege — or perhaps because of it. Valletta's citizens need distraction more than ever. The lobby smells of wax, dust, perfume dabbed too generously to mask worry. In the upper gallery, a boy in short pants stares through the balustrade as if music might turn him into something else. Nurses sit together, hands in their laps, faces worn. British officers in khaki murmur too loudly, grateful and embarrassed by beauty in equal measure. Maltese families spill into boxes with Sunday-best care—polished shoes, patched coats, pride.

Backstage is a kingdom of nerves, rosin and fastened hooks. A dresser fusses at a loose hem. A violinist tightens a bow. Tosca stands in the wings, fingers around her rosary, lips moving—half prayer, half breath-work. She thinks of the packet under the cloth in the basket and feels its weight from across the building; she thinks of the priest's thin voice; she thinks of Mario's paint under his nails. She makes the sign of the cross because it is how she tells her body to obey.

The curtain rises. Her voice uncoils and fills the space. It has weight and light in it both; it climbs to the plaster cherubs and returns warmer. For minutes on end, the war does not exist. Eyes soften; shoulders drop. A British colonel blinks too often, and the nurse beside him pretends not to see.

In a box swallowed by shadows, Captain Scarpia sits with his gloved hands folded on the velvet rail. He does not applaud. He does not need to. He watches as one appraises a fortress, finding faults, ways in.

"She's so beautiful. She sings like an angel," his lieutenant whispers.

"Even angels can fall," Scarpia replies, the corner of his mouth twisting on a thought.

Applause breaks after the aria, echoing around the space. Tosca bows once, twice, smiles with her eyes closed because the world is larger that way. The curtain kisses the stage. The interval is a whirl of whispered comparisons, of programmes folded into fans. Some step into the foyer to stretch their legs.

Tosca slips into the narrow passage that leads to the stage door. The air is cooler here; Old Theatre Street breathes along the crack of the door. A black-veiled nun waits in the shadow, hands hidden in sleeves, a posture that exudes patience, her pale face half-hidden in her wimple.

"You know what to do?" Tosca whispers.

The nun nods once. There is no ceremony. Tosca passes the wicker basket to her. The nun takes it and vanishes into the shadows of blackout street, the door closing silently behind the barest breath of night air. Somewhere outside, a bicycle rattles past on an untrue wheel.

Relief loosens Tosca's spine. Her body wants to sag, but she has another act to sing. She turns toward her dressing room—and stops.

The corridor is narrow, and he fills it. Scarpia's smile, while it's a smile, it exudes iciness. "Brava, signorina," he says, and the softness is an insult. "A performance worthy of angels."

"I didn't expect you tonight," she answers, steady. Her hands are at her sides, relaxed by force.

"I never miss good music," Scarpia says. His gaze glances past her toward the stage door and returns, as if he has sniffed the ghost of a thing and catalogued it. "*In bocca al lupo.*"

He steps aside with a courtly tilt of the head that makes the passage narrower. Tosca goes by, chin level, breathing shallowly through her nose. In the wings, she crosses herself again—not out of superstition but to remind the universe it has rules—and steps back into the light.

Behind her, Scarpia stands in the dimness and listens to an orchestra tune itself into order.

Back in his seat, his lieutenant leans in. "Shall I...?"

"Not yet," Scarpia says, "let her finish the act." He smiles thinly at the cruelty of timing; theatre has taught him when to enter.

The second act unfolds and the audience listens. In the gallery, the short-pants boy watches Tosca's hands and thinks perhaps singing like that needs a lot of exercise. In the stalls, a Maltese mother holds her daughter's fingers in hers, counting them, as if presence must be inventoried during war. A British officer clears his throat and pretends it was dust. The nurse sitting next to him pretends not to hear that.

When the final curtain falls, the room rises to its feet and applause falls like thunder. Tosca takes one bow, two, three—the last with a hand to her heart because the applause feels like a blessing, a blessing she would keep whole and take with her if she could. She backs into the wings with the smile still on as a shield, and only when the curtain is fully down does her face go slack with fatigue.

She thinks of Mario. Of Angelotti, of Malta. She thinks, not for the first time, that the sound of boots marching can follow like a shadow, ominous and ever present.

Outside, the heat and humidity of the day is still in the air in the darkened city. Somewhere already, a door that should not open is opening. The nun is a shadow among shadows, and a basket has become the most important object in Valletta. Upstairs in a *palazzo* that used to host card games and gossip, a desk is cleared of ledgers to make room for maps and orders. In the church where the Madonna still lacks a final glaze of light on the lower lip, a slab sits flush and looks like the stone has sat that way forever.

And onstage, for a few more heartbeats, Tosca is simply a woman catching her breath.

The curfew bells toll outside, deep and urgent. The streets are already beginning to empty.

The Devil's Bargain

The Palazzo Paschal, above the Bakery

Valletta is dark, quiet and holding its breath, hoping for a night without air raids, sleeping lightly to hear sounds of alarm, dreaming of better times. The curfew went into effect at nine-thirty; it is now a little after ten. The streets below are dark and bare as bones, and the blackout makes every window a blind eye. The old *Palazzo Paschal* on the Old Bakery Street now has a bakery that used to feed half the quarter. Tonight, the ovens are cold; flour sacks lean like tired men against the wall; the long wooden peels rest where they were left after the dawn's bake. Only the faint, stale scent of bread lingers—yeast, ash and the memory of warmth.

Upstairs, Scarpia has made the *palazzo* into a *palazzo* again. Candles now shine in sconces polished to a high sheen, oil lamps purr. The room retains its faded grandeur—cracked tiles patterned in a Moorish star, a coffered ceiling painted with saints whose eyes no longer

26

meet yours, a window shuttered tight against the harbour. The desk is covered with neat piles of papers and maps. On a side table, an obscene parade: salami and *prosciutto*, a wedge of hard cheese sweating a little in the heat, a tomato sliced and jewelled with oil and salt, olives in a chipped bowl, a bottle of Sicilian red, breathing. The food announces rank more emphatically than medals.

Scarpia stands by the shuttered window, cigarette glowing, smoke making a slow ribbon that twines with the candlelight. His lieutenant, hat under his arm, waits with the patience of a man who has learned more from silence than from orders.

"The informer saw her, Captain," the lieutenant says. "At the Manoel. Interval. The singer gave a basket to a nun by the stage door. The nun slipped into *Triq Orsla* before our men could get through the crowd."

"And the basket?" Scarpia asks without turning.

"Found later near the harbour, Sir. Empty."

Scarpia flicks ash into a dish. "Empty things can be full of guilt." He smiles a little. "Bring me Cavardossi."

The lieutenant bows and is gone, the door falling shut on a hiss of smoke.

Scarpia turns to the table and pours a finger of wine. He holds the glass up to the candle, tilts it and studies the colour, as if it might tell him the weather of the morning, or the precise point at which another person will break.

The door bangs open on boots and breath. as the Military Police drags Mario Cavardossi in. Their khaki uniforms are dusty from the night's search; armbands marked with the insignia of the Military Police catching the lamplight. Cavardossi's wrists are bruised where hands have held too tightly. The painter's shirt is torn along one seam; paint shadows his knuckles, and a smear of greenish blue has dried on the back of his left hand, a relic from a world with light.

Scarpia looks up from his desk, wineglass in hand. "Well," he said softly, "our painter has arrived."

He gestures to a chair without looking at it. "Sit, *Signor* Cavardossi."

Mario remains standing. He is breathing too fast from the drag up the stairs, and the smell of the table—oil, meat, cheese—hits him like a fist in the gut. He hadn't realised until now how empty his body was; he hasn't eaten since Tosca's sandwiches in the church, hours and miles of fear ago.

"Your men broke into my studio," he says.

"They came with a key known as duty, which you undoubtedly haven't practiced nor heard of." Scarpia sips some wine, the line well-practised. "You are accused of aiding Cesare Angelotti, a fugitive and an enemy of the state, and of passing information to the Italians. You're a traitor."

"That is absurd."

Scarpia sets the glass down, studying the wet print it leaves on the wood. "A witness saw your Tosca hand a basket to a nun last night. The basket was found empty at the harbour. The nun is gone." He raises his eyes at last. "What was in it?"

Mario's mouth waters involuntarily. The shame of it—his body begging at the sight of meat on Scarpia's table—brings bitter taste of bile into his mouth. His stomach makes a small, traitorous sound.

"Food," he says. "For the Sisters of Mercy. They feed orphans while you dine."

"Ah," Scarpia says softly, "charity with nocturnal habits. You expect me to applaud? Malta is full of starving mouths. Do you take Tosca for a delivery girl?"

"For a Christian," Mario snaps. "Have you walked through Floriana at dusk? Children gnaw ration bread like leather. Women trade wedding rings for onions. And yet—" he jerks his chin toward the table, "you— you spread your black-market spoils like a feast day."

Scarpia glances at the table, amused without humour. "Privilege of office, Cavardossi. It could be yours in another life." He tips the bottle and adds a second finger to the glass, then thinks better and slides the glass out of Mario's reach with one languid finger. "But not this one."

Mario spits on the floor. One of the guards shifts with the intent to strike; Scarpia doesn't bother to nod permission.

"Take him below," he says.

The cellar stairs are old. Stone smoothed out by years of use. They sweat. The air down there smells of damp and iron and the sour tang that bodies leave when afraid. A single oil lamp throws a porthole of light that rocks a little when people move around in the closed space.

They strip Mario to the waist and tie him to a post with practised economy. The rope is stained and smooth. He tests the give and finds none. Screaming here is heard by no-one, not even by the Madonna. He lifts his chin and looks at the lamp instead of at the whip.

"Ten," Scarpia says from the doorway, voice conversational, as if ordering bread.

The whip is leather. The first strike is a stripe of fire; the second finds the same place because the arm swinging it has memory. At four his breath goes ragged. At six, his knees tremble. He bites the inside of his cheek and tastes blood. He thinks of light—how it lives in paint even when the world is dark. He thinks of Tosca's hand moving when she sings, the way she opens her fingers on a sustained note as if giving away the sound will make it larger.

On eight he sags. The guard with the bucket steps forward, throws the cold seawater with a brutal force. The sting of the salty water shocks him back into his body.

"Again," Scarpia says, polite as a maître d'.

Nine. Ten.

Mario swallows a cry and loses the swallow in a gasp. The light wobbles, and the room seems to move a fraction to the left.

Scarpia raises a hand. "Enough. Untie him and bring him up." His voice is bored; he has what he came for: a man softened at the edges.

Back upstairs the office feels indecently bright, the smell: sweat, damp stone, and blood — but also wine, smoked meat, and ripe cheese.

Tosca is already there—two guards flanking her at a careful distance, ready to hold her if need be. She stands tall, spine ironed straight by fear. Her face is bloodless except at the mouth, lips red from biting them hard.

"You came," Scarpia said, rising with courtly politeness as though she were a guest rather than a prisoner's lover summoned at night. "How gracious."

On Scarpia's desk sits a wicker basket—the basket—clean, empty, containing Tosca's handkerchief. Placed there carefully, like a relic, by a guard.

Scarpia nods. "Recognise this, *Signorina*?"

Before Tosca can answer, the guard who carried it in speaks, eager for credit. "Found it near the harbour, Captain. Empty. Informer swore he saw the *signorina* hand it to a nun after the performance."

"Yes," Tosca says, clear and quick, stepping forward. "It held bread and cheese I bought from a seller for the

Sisters of Mercy. They feed children—dozens—who have no one."

"At ten o'clock at night?" Scarpia asks, "Really? How extraordinary."

"Hunger does not wait for daylight," Tosca snaps. She cannot help herself, the sight of the table of overflowing with contraband catches in her throat. She croaks and points—her hand shaking with fury, not fear. "Perhaps you should send some of 'that' to the convent, Captain, instead of idly masticating it all by yourself."

For a fleeting heartbeat one of the guards looks down, as if he has found his boots interesting. Scarpia's smile thins to a wire.

"Charity is a virtue," he says. "Obedience is a law. Treason trumps both." He lifts a finger. "Bring him."

They drag Mario in, wet hair plastered to his forehead, shirt clinging to his skin haphazardly. The welts across his back have bled and clotted and bled again where the cloth has rubbed them. He stumbles, and Tosca is there—faster than the guards—catching his weight to her, the small sound she makes is a gasp and a sob. She smells the cellar on him and the iron in the blood and the salt of the thrown water.

"You animal!" she hisses at Scarpia over Mario's shoulder. "You call this justice? He's innocent!"

Scarpia spreads his hands in a parody of grace. "Justice demands answers. He has none to give me. Perhaps you do."

"I know nothing."

"Then he will be returned below," Scarpia says, as if discussing the route of a package.

"No," Tosca cries, and the word echoes. Mario lifts his head, and the look he finds her with is both a plea and a command.

"Don't," he says, voice cracking. "Not for me."

Scarpia watches them as someone does who used to pull the wings of flies: curious, cold. "Brave," he murmurs. "We shall see what another hour does to bravery." He nods. The guards move.

"Mario!" Tosca's voice breaks on his name as they pull him away.

He turns once in the doorway, and she sees all the years they will not have in that blink. The door closes on him like a lid.

Silence follows. The air tick, tick, ticks in Tosca's ears where her pulse lives.

"Of course, he must be seen to be punished. He is accused of treason — there must be a reckoning."

Tosca's hands clench. "You mean to kill him?"

"What do you want?" she says finally. No tremor: the strength comes from a place she didn't know she had until now.

Scarpia sets the basket aside with two fingers, as if clearing a stage. He does not sit behind the desk yet; he likes the angle of looking down, the benefit of commanding height.

"Want?" He lets the word roll around his mouth. "Want is such a simple thing. I want the fugitive Angelotti. Failing that, I want assurance that the British will not be encouraged by leaks. Failing both—" He steps closer until she can see the pores on his cheek where the razor missed, the faint sheen of sweat at the hairline. "—I want you."

Those words drop between them like stones in a well.

Tosca's hand curls at her side. "You disgust me."

"Perhaps," he says, as if the point bears no weight, "but I hold the rope that binds the man you love. It is amazing what disgust will purchase when love is hungry."

She swallows. The room smells too strongly of food and wax; the basket on the desk is a relic of hope turned into evidence; her heart pounds her ribs.

"What guarantees?" she asks. "Words weigh nothing with you."

His thin lips curl. "A practical woman." He goes behind the desk at last and sits, the chair creaking like a complaint. He draws a sheet of paper toward him and a pen. "Of course he must be 'seen' to be executed," Scarpia says, conversationally, "he is accused of treason after all. Malta needs its theatre. But for you, that can be arranged to end without a death. I will order blanks at dawn." He looks up with narrowing his eyes and tilting his head, a look that only convinces the weak and the desperate. "On my honour."

Tosca's laugh is a short, broken thing. "What honour can live in your mouth?"

"The only honour that matters," he says, dipping the pen, "is the one stamped with my seal." He writes. His hand is elegant, even, unhurried. His signature lavish. He enjoys the movement of ink on paper, the power in watching letters become words, words creating orders. When he finishes the mock-execution order, he grabs the elegantly engraved silver ink blotter to blot the ink dry. He takes a second sheet. "And to show my good will, a safe-conduct for you both. You will go to the harbour after dawn; I will have the guard stand aside. You may sail wherever wind and war allow."

Tosca stands very still, as if any movement might knock over what she is building inside herself: a bridge between survival and sin. She hears Mario's voice in her head—'Don't, not for me'—and answers him in thought: 'for you, because there is no world without you in it.' She hears, beneath that, the priest's thin warning: 'the devil himself walked through this church.' She looks at the table of overflowing with food and thinks, without knowing why, 'this is the devil's banquet.'

Scarpia blots the second sheet. He places both papers side by side and leans back, admiring the neat parallel as if he has lined up twins. "With these," he says softly, "you are free."

The room is so quiet she can hear a fly test the edge of a window shutter. Tosca's hands, which can conjure a phrase out of thin air and hold hundreds silent, are empty. She walks past the desk, pauses at the side table. The tomato bleeds a little onto the plate; the knife that cut it lies besides it small and sharp, its edge catching a filament of candlelight.

She closes her fingers around the knife. Its weight is barely there and absolute, her hand behind her back.

She circles the table as if looking for something to eat, a woman restless after a bad dinner party. Scarpia watches her with feline patience. He thinks his mouse is ready.

Tosca moves swiftly, years of training on stage, approaching his left side, slightly behind him, as any supplicant might be, reaching to see the papers. She leans forward, her right hand masked by her body, breath held so hard her ribs ache.

"Shall we seal our bargain?" Scarpia says, voice low, tender with triumph.

Her right arm flashes, fast as a stage cue, sure as a remembered aria. The knife goes into the right side of his neck, deep, severing what must be severed if a man is to be unmade quickly. Blood pours out, dark where it crosses the white of the paper. He makes a guttural sound and lurches forward, both hands flying to where his life runs out.

Before he can find the breath to shout, she strikes again, thrusting the blade into the base of his skull, a short, brutal motion that empties the body of will. He convulses once. The wineglass tips, the red fractures into beads across the desk and drops, a dark spill. The chair scrapes and stills. The room is layered with silence.

Tosca steps back, her chest heaving. The knife is still in her hand. She hasn't realised she still held it. She sets it down carefully on the table beside the tomato, the blade laid parallel to the slice as if that was important.

She crosses herself slowly, deliberately, as if teaching her body the gesture again. "Lord," she whispers, and the word is made of gravel, "forgive me this violent act. I had no other way." She leans toward the slack head on the desk and adds, voice low and steady, "Fare well, Captain—straight to the devil who waits for you."

She notices her hands are slick. She wipes them on the linen tablecloth. The act steadies her. She reaches across Scarpia's body, picks up both papers—the mock-execution order and the safe-conduct—folds them with care and tucks them into her bodice, where the beat of her heart marks time against the crackle of paper.

"Now we are free," she says softly, and is surprised to find her voice can still produce words.

She straightens her dress, squares her shoulders to make her exit. Tosca looks at the room once more. The candle gutters. The blood stains the carpet. The basket looks ordinary again, a thing for bread and small mercies.

She walks to the door and opens it a little, just enough for her to exit.

"The Captain is not to be disturbed," she tells the guard, composed as ever. "He has retired for the night."

The guard, who has never been this close to her before, nods.

She closes the door quietly behind her and starts down the stairs. The banister is smooth with the hands of a century of people who likely never had to do what she has done. Below, the bakery smells of yesterday morning. She pauses, just long enough to feel that her legs will carry her and steps out into the night.

In the guard office below a tired Maltese lieutenant waits with a ledger and a conscience that has started to get his attention. He hears the murmur of a woman's voice from above, then nothing. When Tosca passes, he sees only a lady moving with grace and calm, with elegance that makes him want to doff his cap.

He goes upstairs, knocks at Scarpia's door and waits the exact count a subordinate learns. No answer. He knocks again. Stillness. It is not his business to open the door of a superior who wishes not to be disturbed; it is his business to carry out orders already given.

He goes back down, to his ledger, finds the line that matters: -Dawn. Fort St Elmo. Prisoner Cavardossi to be shot for treason. – Scarpia ensured, the Treachery Act from 1940 is clear on this matter. He swallows the taste of blood in his mouth and signs for the squad.

Outside, the city is starting to wake for another day. Somewhere far off, a rooster—confused by blackout and war—misplaces the hour.

On the Bastion

Dawn

S un is about to come up. The early morning light paints the limestone a pale ghostly blue. The Grand Harbour lies still and metallic, a single British destroyer at anchor like a hulking beast, asleep, but ready. Coal smoke curls from a single stack somewhere below, thin as a pencil line. A gull cries, solitary, and the sound seems to hang still in the humid air before dropping away. It's going to be hot.

Fort St Elmo is almost silent. The bastion gravel crunches under the boots of the small firing squad forming near the parapet. Rifles gleam in the half-light, bayonets glint briefly as they are checked. The men work with the automatic quiet of soldiers who have done this before and dislike it.

The Maltese lieutenant in charge checks his watch. The movement catches the light, and he slips it back into his tunic with a small sigh. He has been awake most of the night — waiting, smoking, thinking about what will be required of him at dawn. His face is drawn, jaw tight. This is war, he thinks. Just following orders, he thinks.

The heavy door below creaks and Cavardossi is led out between two guards. He is barefoot now, shirt clinging to his body where blood has dried in dark stripes from the flogging. His hair is damp from the bucket thrown over him to wake him; his skin looks almost translucent in the early morning light.

They allow him to sit on a stone bench near the wall while preparations are finished. The bench is cold, seeping into his bones, but he is too exhausted to care. He leans back and tips his head toward the awakening sky.

For a moment, with the harbour wind on his face, he can almost pretend he is just waiting for the sun to rise, for the day's work to begin, for the ladders to be set against the wall of the church so he might paint again.

He draws a slow breath and lets it out. The air is sharp with salt. Somewhere far down in the city a baker is stoking an oven, and the smell of wood-smoke drifts faintly up toward the bastion. Hunger twists in his stomach, but along with it comes something stranger — a sudden, bittersweet pleasure at still being alive, at tasting the air one last time.

He thinks of Tosca. The sound of her voice seems to float in the empty air: the Manoel filled with her singing, the whole theatre hushed. He remembers her teasing jealousy in the church, the fierce flash of her eyes. He remembers her hands passing him sandwiches with mock severity, telling him even saints must eat.

A half-smile pulls at his mouth. She was angry with him then. *Will she think kindly of him when he is gone? Perhaps she will escape Malta, find a way to Spain or Portugal, anywhere beyond the reach of this war. Perhaps she will sing again for a theatre full of people who have never seen a siege.*

Angelotti's face appears in his mind, ghostly pale as he slipped into the crypt. *Did he make it beyond Valletta's walls? Or was he caught before the night ended?* Mario whispers a quick prayer, almost unconsciously, for the man and for the others in the network who risk everything.

His fingers trace the edge of the stone, rough and pitted. He feels strangely calm now. The fear has passed; only a clarity remains. He will die soon — he can taste it, a metallic certainty — but he hopes Tosca will live. Let her voice survive this war, he thinks. Let her voice survive me.

He closes his eyes and lifts his face toward the sky. The first faint warmth of the rising sun touches his eyelids. If this is his last morning, let it be painted in gold.

Footsteps echo on the stairs. He opens his eyes, thinking perhaps the end has come — and then he sees her.

Tosca appears at the top of the steps, a dark silhouette against the growing light. She is breathless from the climb, hair pinned hastily, but her face is lit with fierce triumph. She holds two folded papers like talismans.

She crosses herself quickly before stepping into the open air, then strides straight to the lieutenant, holding out the first paper.

"Captain Scarpia's order," she says, her voice still quick from running. "A mock execution — blanks only."

The lieutenant takes it, opens it carefully, scans the writing. His jaw works once, and something tightens in his face. He folds the paper again and slips it into his pocket.

He doesn't speak.

Tosca doesn't wait for his answer. She hurries to Mario and drops to her knees beside him, clutching him fiercely.

"It is done!" she gasps, her breath warm against his neck. "Scarpia himself signed it. They will fire blanks, Mario — blanks! You must fall as though dead, and then we will go to the harbour together. Look — here!"

She pulls the second paper from her bodice and shows him the safe-conduct, still blotched with Scarpia's blood.

Mario smiles, faint but real, and cups her cheek with his rough hand, leaving a smear of red on her skin.

"You are a miracle, Tosca," he whispers.

They cling together, heads close, their words tumbling over each other. She tells him of the bargain, of Scarpia's last breath, of how she knelt and prayed forgiveness before she fled.

"I told him to travel to the devil," she says fiercely.

Mario presses his forehead to hers. "Brave, my Tosca. Braver than any soldier I know."

Behind them, the lieutenant exhales and glances at the sky. The sun is rising fast now. He crosses himself quickly, then calls, "Form up!"

The squad takes position in a line, boots grinding on the gravel. The sergeant checks each man, adjusts the spacing with quiet efficiency. The soldiers look grim; no one speaks.

Tosca helps Mario to his feet, her hands gentle as she steadies him.

"Remember, my love," she says softly, "you must fall well — like on stage. Fall slowly — make them believe it."

Mario manages a short laugh, though his throat is tight. "If this is to be my last performance, I will play it for you."

He kisses her quickly, tasting the salt of her tears.

The lieutenant raises his voice. "Ready!"

The soldiers lift their rifles. The metallic clatter of bolts being drawn back is sharp and final.

Tosca takes a few steps back, pressing her hands to her ears, turning her face away.

"Present arms!"

"Fire!"

The loud noise shatters the dawn quiet, echoing against the stone and out across the harbour.

Mario's body jerks once and collapses to the gravel.

For a heartbeat there is perfect silence.

Then Tosca lets out the breath she has been holding and rushes forward, smiling through tears. "Mario! It is over — get up! Quick, quick, before they change their minds!"

She pulls at his arm. His body is limp.

Her smile falters.

"Mario?"

She presses her ear to his chest, feels for the flutter of a pulse, the rise of breath. Her hands come away wet. The smell of blood hits her.

"No," she whispers. "No, no, no..."

She shakes him, first gently, then with gathering panic. "Mario, wake up! The bullets were to be blanks — you must get up — you must—"

But his head lolls against her arm. His eyes are half-lidded, staring at nothing.

The truth surges through her like a sharp knife. "Noooooooooo!" she cries. "Scarpia lied!" Her voice is raw. "He lied — and I believed him!"

She collapses across Mario, clutching him to her as though sheer will might warm him again. Her sobs tear at the air.

"You cannot leave me," she whispers. "I killed for you. I prayed for you. Don't leave me alone in this hell."

Shouts from the stairwell: "Captain Scarpia is dead — murdered!"

Scarpia's Military Police storm onto the rampart, rifles raised, boots ringing on the stone.

"There!" one of them shouts, pointing at Tosca. "She was the last to see him alive!"

The soldiers of the firing squad look at one another uneasily. Some step back, unsure where loyalty ends and justice begins.

"Stay where you are!" the sergeant barks.

Tosca rises slowly from where she has been kneeling by Mario's body. Her face is pale and streaked with tears, her hands still sticky with his blood. She looks around at the circle closing in, at the rifles pointed her way, at the harbour just beginning to glow with morning light.

"You will not have me," she says quietly, almost to herself.

She backs toward the parapet, never taking her eyes off the soldiers. No one moves to grab her — perhaps out of shock, perhaps out of some small respect.

At the edge she pauses, her breath coming steady now. She glances down at Mario one last time, memorising the angle of his face, the dark curls against the stone.

Her lips move silently — a prayer, a farewell.

Then, without haste, she climbs onto the parapet, skirt brushing the damp stone, glances below and lets herself fall forward into the empty air.

The soldiers shout and rush to the edge; but it is too late.

Below, morning mist curls over the lower streets of Valletta. Far away, there is the faint sound of something striking stone, then silence.

The lieutenant removes his cap, crosses himself slowly, and mutters, "God have mercy on her soul."

Coda

The squad begins to lift Cavardossi's body. As they roll him onto a stretcher, a folded paper slips from beneath him — the safe-conduct Tosca had shown him so proudly.

The lieutenant bends down, picks it up. It is stained with blood, the ink blurred, but still legible.

He reads it once, jaw tightening, then folds it carefully and tucks it into his tunic.

"So much blood," he mutters.

He gives the order to carry the body away. The bugle sounds faintly from the barracks, calling the city to another day.

Dawn breaks fully, washing the bastion in gold — a cruel, bright light for the dead and the living alike.

Valletta begins to waken — carts rattling on cobble-stones, shutters opening, the cries of vendors. The world moves forward, unaware that two lovers lie dead because of one man's lies.

Epilogue

By mid-morning, word has spread through Valletta. The cafés on Strada Reale buzz with low voices among the ration lines.

In the *Times of Malta*, a brief notice appears under the military communique:

> DISTURBANCE–
> OFFICER DEAD
> Captain Baron Vitale
> Scarpia, head of the
> Maltese Military
> Police, was found
> slain in his office late
> last night. An
> investigation is
> ongoing.

No mention in the paper of Tosca, nor of Cavardossi's execution, but by noon, every alley in Valletta knows the story. Mothers hold their children a little closer. Priests say quiet prayers over morning Mass.

"They shot him at dawn," someone whispered — a stevedore in a dusty cap. "Executed him, the Painter, Cavardossi. Claimed he was a traitor."

"A traitor? He was no traitor! He restored the Madonna at St Paul's—"

"And the singer — Tosca — jumped from St Elmo's bastion. They say she flew like an angel."

In the silence of the harbour mist, their love ended as the sun broke over the city — a requiem written in stone and blood.

THE END

THE BASTION PROTOCOL

Three Gates, One Man,

No Time to Fail.

A.K. LAKELETT

Faukon Abbey Publishing

Contents

THE
BASTION
PROTOCOL

THREE GATES, ONE MAN, NO TIME TO FAIL

BOOK 2 IN BASTION TRILOGY

A.K. LAKELETT

Prologue
Flight to Valletta

The plane jolted as it banked over the Mediterranean. From his window seat, Calaf could see Malta appear like a stone ship rising out of the sea, the bastions of Valletta glowing amber in the late sun.

He hadn't been on Maltese soil in five years. Not since the MI6 job that ended his career — and nearly ended him.

He closed his eyes and let the hum of the engines drown out the memories. It didn't work.

He had sworn off this life. Sworn off operations, intrigue, the endless games. But three weeks ago, a message had found him in London – short, brutal, and impossible to ignore.

No signature, no trace, just sixteen words and a date:

> **Annex B confirmed.**
>
> **Malta compromised.**
>
> **You still know where the bodies**

are buried.

Go to Valletta.

Annex B. The leaked drafts of the China–Malta treaty had been public for months, but no one had seen Annex B — a "data corridor arrangement" that would allegedly give Beijing privileged access to Malta's digital infrastructure, and by extension, a potential backdoor into EU banking corridors. Rumours that it existed abounded, without confirmation.

He had sworn off intelligence work after London. Burned his bridges. Quit the Service. Told himself he was done playing the game.

And yet, here he was. Ticket in hand, cover story filed as "independent journalist". Because the truth was, he wanted back in.

The captain's voice came over the intercom, announcing the descent into Luqa. Calaf leaned back and watched as Malta came into view — a stone citadel rising from the sea, its honey-coloured bastions blazing under the late-afternoon sun.

Malta had always been a crossroads. Phoenicians, Ottomans, the Knights of St. John, the French, the British Empire — all had turned the island into a fortress. Now it was Europe's southern firewall, hosting FinTech servers and AI research labs, quietly handling traffic too sensitive for Frankfurt or Paris.

Which made it a perfect target.

Liu's face came back to him as the plane descended.

They had worked together before, back when he was still a "clean" intelligence analyst. She had been one of the few who believed whistleblowers could actually fix a system instead of just burning it down. After he left the Service, she'd stayed, quietly shifting into consultancy roles with parliamentary access.

Two days ago, she'd messaged him:

> **Meet me in Valletta.**
>
> **Annex B is real.**
>
> **If this treaty passes,**
>
> **we lose control of the**
>
> **island's backbone.**
>
> **I can get you proof**
>
> **— but you'll have to do the rest.**

She had always trusted him more than he trusted himself. That was why he was on this flight.

And then there was Turandot Vassallo.

He had read about her on social media and in the press – some fawning, some fearful: Daughter of the Prime Minister of Malta. Cambridge-trained prodigy, cryptographer, degrees from Zurich and MIT. Architect of Malta's cyber-defence strategy. She had built the Bastion Protocol almost single-handedly; a failsafe, self-healing architecture designed to keep Malta's core systems and infrastructure alive even under siege, and by extension others who used it as well.

Some called her a saviour. Others called her an ice queen with a beautiful face, an elitist genius who treated democracy like a variable to be managed. Some called her Malta's Ada Lovelace. She had once solved a NATO white-hat challenge in under an hour, leaving her competitors humiliated and forcing the organisers to pull the plug to avoid embarrassment.

Calaf had never met her. But he had met others like her — those who believed that if you controlled the system, you controlled the world.

He wasn't sure if he was flying to Valletta to stop her, outsmart her — or to see if she could still be reached.

His father's voice came back to him — Timur, former diplomat, now living in quiet exile on Gozo: *"Small nations don't survive by strength. They survive by leverage. Malta always sells its value to the highest bidder. Watch who she sells it to next."*

The plane jolted on landing, tires screaming against the runway.

As they taxied toward the terminal, Calaf powered on his phone. One message waited for him on the secure app:

FROM: UNKNOWN

SUBJECT:WELCOME BACK

Parliament

watchers are

nervous.

Liu is inside.

Treaty vote

in ten days.

Watch the daughter.

She holds the key.

Calaf smiled grimly.

He didn't need the message to tell him that.

Turandot Vassallo had built a fortress.

And if the fortress was locked with riddles, he intended to be the man who solved them.

The First Gate

V alletta smells of wet limestone and sea salt. The streets glisten from an afternoon shower, and the crowd that moves along Republic Street is a mixture of tourists, civil servants heading home, and protesters chanting against the upcoming Malta–China treaty.

Calaf keeps his head low, his messenger bag pressed against his side, collar up. He's been in Valletta for three days, and he already feels the island is a chessboard — one where the pieces are shifting faster than anyone can see.

As early afternoon leans across the city, the bastions glowing like banked coals, and the street outside the Mediterranean Conference Centre hums with the low static of people who know things they won't say in public.

Calaf moves with the flow. He stops at the foot of the stairs leading to the Mediterranean Conference Centre. A banner above the entrance boldly proclaims:

BASTION
PROTOCOL
MALTA'S FUTURE
IN CYBERSECURITY

He clocks the plaza quickly — plainclothes at the edges; a camera mast aimed at the entrance; a knot of aides in navy suits whose earpieces flash a faint green when they tap them. On Republic Street, protestors pack away their placards: **NO SECRET ANNEX**, **WE ARE NOT A CORRIDOR**. A woman with a bullhorn takes a last photo, then rubs her face like she's washing off the day.

He blends in. Badge pickup. Smile. The volunteer scans the QR code he generated that morning. Green tick, temporary badge: *MEDIA — INDEPENDENT.*

"Down the corridor, sir," the volunteer says, bright and bored. "Main hall. Phones on silent, please."

Perfect cover.

In the foyer, sponsors push coffee and promises. A screen loops a promo: Malta as keystone—undersea cables converging, container ships and data packets sliding like schools of fish, the Bastion logo superimposed on Valletta walls.

Inside, the atmosphere buzzes with restrained excitement. Cybersecurity experts, diplomats, politicians, and government aides take their seats in the main hall. The stage is stark: a long table with microphones, a giant screen displaying the Bastion logo — a stylised outline of Valletta's walls with three interlocking gates — and, at the centre, a solitary podium.

He takes an aisle seat in the last row, back to the wall. Old habit. The hall is dark wood and discreet LEDs. The government press desk sits up front, note-takers already typing. On the other side of the aisle, a blond man in a navy suit meets his eyes, then looks away. Noted. A blond man in Malta where everyone is mostly dark - haired, seems like an odd choice for a watchdog, Calaf thinks.

The room goes quiet. She walks onto the stage.

Turandot Vassallo.

She's younger than he'd expected — late twenties, perhaps — but her bearing is anything but youthful. The stage lights flatten out everyone else, but they sharpen her—tall, raven-haired, dressed in black trousers and a pale blue silk blouse, she carries herself with the self-possession of someone who's spent her life being the smartest person in every room. She hadn't looked at the audience as she crossed to the podium. She doesn't need to.

"Malta is small," she says by way of opening, her voice clear, accented lightly with Maltese vowels but perfectly international. "But small states survive by thinking ahead. Today I present the Bastion Protocol — a failsafe cryptographic architecture designed to keep Malta's critical infrastructure beyond the reach of cyberattack."

Behind her, the screen lights up: threat maps, heat blobs, a knotted skein of under-sea cables through the Sicilian Channel.

Calaf finds himself leaning forward.

"A nation's arteries are glass and light," she says. "Ports, banks, traffic control, hospital oxygen, card terminals at your local pastizzeria—interrupt any two, and you have chaos. The Bastion Protocol is a failsafe cryptographic architecture to hold the core when everything else is under attack." She talks for more than an hour, with no paper, no need to check her talking points.

She keeps it technical enough that dignitaries nod without understanding. Calaf can feel the room's current; it shifts with each term she drops—threshold signatures, lattice-based primitives, HSMs air-gapped in a temperature-controlled vault. Theatre for the faithful; intimidation for everyone else.

Then she smiles, tightly and mercilessly.

"Malta is a democracy," she says, letting the word ride. "We will prove our system through adversarial testing. The Bastion is locked by three riddles. Each is based on a historical moment that defines Malta's survival — from the Great Siege to the Second World War. Solve them, and you may open the Bastion to observe its design. Fail, and you will be permanently blacklisted from every EU cybersecurity tender for the next decade."

A ripple runs through the audience. Fear, seasoned with appetite. She has turned national security into a game with career-level stakes.

"No one has solved even the first," she adds, slicing through hope, "but Malta is nothing if not democratic. I invite challengers."

Silence. A cough. The rustle of people suddenly fascinated by their programmes.

Calaf stands up. Two chairs scrape near the aisle—security clocking movement. He keeps his hands visible.

"Name?" an aide calls from the side.

"Calaf," he says. "Independent journalist."

This raises eyebrows. A hush folds over the row around him, the way a flock tightens when a hawk passes. Journalists cover such matters; they don't step into them.

Turandot looks at him properly now—as one might examine an unexpected variable in a systems test.

"A journalist? This is not a press conference," she says. "This is national security."

"I thought Malta was democratic," Calaf says, smiling. "Or is that just for the banner?"

A few engineers risk brief smiles quickly suppressed. Turandot's eyes cool, then sharpen as if she's decided: all right, then. Let's see.

She inclines her head slightly. "Very well, step forward," she says.

He moves down the aisle, messenger bag against his hip. The blond in navy tracks him, thumb along his jaw as if suppressing irritation. Plainclothes one, almost certainly. Good. Calaf walks to the microphone set up at the side of the hall. His pulse is a steady hammer, but his mind is clear.

At the side mic, Calaf rests his notepad on the stand. The stage lights turn the hall into a dark sea with islands of faces.

"The first riddle," Turandot says, voice taking on a formal cadence, "concerns Malta's survival during its darkest hour."

The screen changes to a blue text box, displaying a short paragraph:

> *My cradle is wind and stone,*
> *My words ride on storms*
> *though I have no breath.*
> *Three letters hear me*
> *before the island sleeps,*
> *And through me the*
> *hawk strikes first.*
> *What am I?*

Murmurs ripple outward. It's the sort of thing half the room wants to Google; half of that half already knows their phones are broadcasting.

Calaf flips his notepad, pencil moving.

My cradle is wind + stone= cliffs? **Dingli?** (underlines it twice)

My words ride on storms though I have no breath = transmission without breath? → **radio?**

Three letters hear me... Three-letter org. Not MI5, not SIS, that would be British, not Maltese. Ah yes, WWII SIGINT jargon: Y. *"Hear me"* is precise. Then it clicked: during WWII, signals intelligence sites were called **Y-Stations** — "Y" for "wireless interception."

And through me the hawk strikes first Air scramble. Spitfires off Ta' Qali, launched before the Luftwaffe reached Malta thanks to early warnings — airborne before radar? Malta had radar, yes, but the earliest warnings often came from HF intercept off Sicily. Dingli listening post, feeding the fighter ops room under the Lascaris bastions.

Calaf speaks before the adrenaline can turn to shakes. He looks at Turandot.

"It's the wireless interception post at Dingli Cliffs," he says clearly.

A pause.

Turandot tilts her head slightly, "Explain your reasoning". Calaf nearly smiles. She wants more than a lucky guess.

"It's the wireless interception post at Dingli Cliffs," he says again. "Wind and stone are the cliffs; 'words without breath' are radio. Three letters' is the Y-Stations' Y for wireless interception that fed intercepts to Malta's defence. Hawk strikes first' is Malta's fighters scrambling ahead of Luftwaffe raids thanks to those intercepts."

The audience is astounded and whispering.

A longer silence now. Not uncertainty—calculation. The government row is deciding how they feel about being outriddled by a freelancer in the first ten minutes.

Turandot's lips curve in the faintest of smiles. Her eyes warm by half a degree.

"Explain how you know the Y-Service, Mr Calaf."

Not a request. A flex. She wants to hear the deduction; she wants to know whether he guessed or *understood*.

"The name," he says, keeping it brisk. "They were called Y-Stations across the British network. Dingli picked up HF chatter off Sicily. With that, and GL radar at Wardi-ja—"

"—and with Lascaris plotting beneath the bastions," she finishes, not to be outdone. She nods slowly, delivering a verdict. "Correct," she says.

Applause starts—first scattered, then bolder when the room realises a trapdoor is not about to open under his feet. Calaf lets his shoulders drop down. *Don't look like you needed the approval. Don't look like you care.*

Turandot waves her hand. The blue box slides away. The Bastion logo turns; the first of the three gates' shades goes from pale to dark as if acknowledging the unlocking.

"You have opened Gate One," she says. "Return at noon tomorrow. You will receive access to the second riddle. Twenty-four hours. No extensions."

"I'll be here," Calaf says.

Something like a smile ghosts the corner of her mouth. Not charming. Competitive.

"See that you are," she says, and lets the applause close for her.

The hall unspools into corridors and networking—the soft hell of conferences everywhere. In the foyer, glossy brochures guard a tray of pastizzi that look like they died bravely.

Calaf hangs at the edge of a cluster where a senior civil servant with a Churchill jaw explains to a foreign attaché why blacklisting is *necessary* in a small market, and anyway, the best people don't mind.

"Mr Calaf," someone says behind him. Male, Maltese, mid-thirties wearing a good suit and the kind of smile a snake would have if it smiled. The blond man from the hall stands just over his shoulder.

"Justin Debrincat," the man says, offering a hand. "Policy advisor. Prime Minister's office."

They shake hands. Debrincat's grip is dry. The man's eyes are as warm as a bowl of ice.

"Impressive answer," Debrincat says. "Journalists don't usually win games they didn't set up."

"I'm not fond of games," Calaf says.

"And yet—" The smile widens a millimetre. "May I ask how you'll be covering the Bastion? We've had... sensationalism. People don't understand what's at stake."

"I write what's there," Calaf says. "If it's sensational, that isn't on me."

"Of course," Debrincat says, his smile stifled like snuffed out match. "Do keep us apprised of any... unusual inquiries, won't you?"

The man shifts so his jacket falls open just enough to show the bulge at his belt. Not a gun; this isn't that kind of room. More likely a jammer or a scrambler. A reminder that he can make your phone forget who it is. So, PM's attack dog, not a plain clothes official.

Calaf excuses himself with a nod and slides out.

Outside Valletta has grown dark, the bastions glowing gold under floodlights. Walking in Valletta at night is perfect for thinking. The alleys hold sound like breath. Cruise passengers have left. Other tourists are eating and drinking at Merchant Street restaurants. Lamps burn behind louvred shutters; music leaks from a door on Strait Street; two boys who should be at home are trying to master a handrail with a skateboard and a prayer.

Calaf climbs to St. George's Square, where the last of the protestors are dispersing. He finds a quiet bench under the arcades and opens his phone.

One message, encrypted, waits in the dead-drop app, sender masked, but fingerprint is obvious. Timur never uses a word he can't repeat under oath.

> **FROM: TIMUR**
> **SUBJECT: ANNEX B**
> **Not public.**

> **Banking corridors +**
>
> **data sharing.**
>
> **Backdoor access,**
>
> **EU not briefed.**
>
> **Find Liu. She has access.**
>
> **Trust no one else**
>
> **Don't call me.**

Calaf exhales slowly. So, his father has been following this all along.

He studies the last line longer than he should, then deletes the message and the app. A church bell tower is just visible over rooftops. He'd told himself he was done being a spy. Perhaps he is. Today felt like something else. A different kind of hunt.

The square's EU flag cracks in a gust. Rain again before dawn.

He meets Liu. She's told him where and when. Her message was written in the sort of careful English that says she can write fluently in two other languages and doesn't trust either of them on open channels.

Café on Old Theatre Street. Eight minutes before eight. She sits at a window table with her back to the wall and a cup of coffee she's let go cold. Early thirties, hair in a loose bun, glasses perched on her nose, chosen to make her invisible in committee rooms. While her beige suit is of the rack, it fits her, and it's perfectly pressed.

"You were very reckless today," she says, stirring her coffee without looking at him.

"Good evening to you too," he says, sitting.

"Being bold and reckless *works* here," she says, "until it doesn't. You'll know the moment it doesn't by the way everyone suddenly becomes interested in your calendar."

He smiles. "Are you interested in my calendar?"

"I'm interested in Annex B." She slides a small flash-drive across the table. It's taped inside a folded café receipt. "This is a preamble draft and the cover sheet. Enough to prove it exists. Not enough to publish without being sued into the sea."

"And the full text?"

"In the Parliament archives. Air-gapped. I can't get it out on my own."

"Why are you doing this?" he asks, even though he already knows the answer; it is always the same answer when good people have had enough.

"Because we are not a corridor," she says, pushing up her glasses. "Because I believe Malta shouldn't become a pawn. Because I like this country more than some of the people running it do. And because you used to believe the same thing, before you left your other job."

Her words sting more than he would have thought possible. He doesn't show his real reaction. She sees it anyway. Efficient people don't waste time pretending they haven't.

"Tomorrow," she says, standing. "Win your second riddle. Then we talk again. Security noticed you today."

"How?"

"Because you were the only person in the room who didn't try to take a selfie with a minister," she says dryly, and leaves.

The coworking space off Merchant Street rents desks by the hour. The receptionist doesn't care who you are as long as your card clears. He picks a desk which offers sight lines to the entrance and a wall at his back, then pulls a clean laptop from his bag—the one with nothing on it except what he inputs there each morning and deletes each night.

He boots cold, kills Wi-Fi. He slips the flash drive Liu gave him into the air-gapped laptop. Password prompt. He types a guess: the parliamentary system name he knows she uses. The file opens — and immediately asks for a second passphrase.

She's clever. The second phrase is buried in the receipt she taped the drive inside. The date stamp is in ISO format — too neat. The seconds field is off by three, a tell. He subtracts three seconds, hashes the new string, feeds it back.

Success. He starts reading more details about Annex B. It's far worse than he had thought.

Later that night, Calaf walks through the Upper Barrakka Gardens, looking out over the Grand Harbour, where the tanker *Ohio* had limped in more than eighty years ago. Below, cranes and container ships gleam in the electric light — Malta's new lifeblood, just as vulnerable to blockade as ever, but now by code rather than bombs.

Somewhere behind one of those bastioned walls, Turandot is waiting. And for reasons he doesn't want to examine too closely, he wants to see that look on her face again — the one she gave him when he solved her riddle.

Tomorrow, he thinks. Tomorrow we'll see how deep this game goes.

Second Gate

V alletta wakes to the smell of rain-wet stone dust. Calaf rises early. He walks into a coffee shop. And again, there seems to be some who take an exceptional interest in him. He takes his time, gets a second cup of coffee, a croissant, and reads the news, Times of Malta, The Guardian, New York Times. Only Times of Malta is reporting on the Bastion Conference. The Guardian only shows an older story about it. He finishes his coffee and starts walking slowly down to the Mediterranean Conference Centre.

It's half-past eleven when reaches the MCC. In the corridor, a woman in a headset is writing names on a list and checking them off with the sort of authority people obey without thinking. His badge is checked again.

Today the hall is fuller; word of his success yesterday has spread. The hall quiets down. Turandot enters last, as if she has been somewhere where numbers behave.

She doesn't ask for his name this time.

"Mr Calaf," she says, courtesy honed like a blade. "You opened Gate One. Are you prepared to return tomorrow with a solution — for Gate Two?"

"I wouldn't be here if I wasn't."

A fractional nod—acknowledgement of nerve, if not respect. She gestures to the screen behind her: the Bastion logo's first gate now dark, the other two pale and waiting.

She produces a sealed envelope, thick as a schoolboy's essay.

"You have until noon tomorrow," she says. "No phones, no outside help, no pleading for hints."

He breaks the seal. Inside: a single sheet of paper and a small, generic USB stick. The screen behind her brightens with the same poem as on the paper—no, not a poem, not quite. A riddle sketched like a sonar return.

Born of iron,
fed by sea,
I came when Malta's
breath was thin.
My coming turned
defeat to hope.
Who am I?

The hall is very quiet, as if every person in it has done the same math: this is about the war; this is about salvation; this is about the convoy. But Turandot never leaves a single thread; she weaves traps into her knots.

Calaf doesn't answer. Let the room think this is theatre. Keep the real work elsewhere.

"Tomorrow noon," he says, folding the page, "you'll have your answer."

Turandot's mouth curves—not approval, not yet, but the professional appreciation of a worthy opponent who refuses to dance on command.

"If you fail," she says, sweet as acid, "you forfeit the game. And your reputation."

"Then I won't fail," he says, and it's not bravado, though his heart is pounding.

The session disperses for lunch in a swirl of linen and lanyards. Calaf goes the other way, toward the stage edge. Two aides slide reflexively to block him. Turandot lifts a finger; they melt aside.

"Why riddles?" he asks, softly. The hall crackles with chatter; their words sit in its shadow.

"Because Malta learns by siege," she says. "We rehearse endurance."

"That sounds like an invitation."

"It's a test."

"Of what?"

"Trust," she says, so quietly he almost misses it.

She steps away before he can answer, swallowed by suits.

As he turns, he feels, rather than sees the PM's assistant in navy stand from two rows back and follow him out. He measures his steps so he won't seem to hurry.

Calaf shoulders through a knot of guests, keeping his badge visible, and peels left into a service stair. The guy follows, then hesitates at the top when a catering trolley wedges into the doorway, silver domes rattling like bells. Calaf descends into cool concrete and exits onto an alley that smells of refuse bags and frying pastry.

He buys a pastizzi from a kiosk because it is there, and because he is a man who always remembers to do something ordinary in the middle of operations; it helps you think, and if anyone is watching, it helps you look like someone who doesn't know he's being watched.

The USB sits cold and heavy in his pocket like a coin he can't spend yet.

Two blocks later, he senses them: not sloppy—two men in casual jackets, mirrored spacing; a scooter lingering; a van idling with lights off. Not the police; they'd have stopped him openly. Watchers, logging routes and faces.

He cuts through a church courtyard, shuffles under a stone arch older than most countries, then skirts the edge of Hastings Gardens to a lane that smells of yesterday's dinners. Finds his way back to the coworking space on Merchant Street again.

He again picks a desk by the wall, away from the window, but with a view of the entrance, then pulls his laptop from his bag—the one with nothing on it.

He boots the laptop, kills the Wi-Fi, and starts the sandboxed environment. Once it's up, he plugs in the USB with the riddle. An encrypted message, a simple interface, a passphrase prompt blinking like an eye.

The paper from the envelope—two lines, capital letters:

NQZVA-PNYY-
QRARENY

1942-08-15

Calaf stares. Not random — not if Turandot has written it.

He laughs once, quietly. ROT13 is a child's lock—good, because it's so bad no one thinks you'll use it. He runs it through a tiny local script.

ADMIZ-CALL-
DGENERAL
1942-08-15

He writes *ADMIZ* and stares. It is almost *ADMIRAL* with letters missing and wrong. *CALL D GENERAL* wants to be an anagram; he shuffles it, impatient. CAL L D GENERAL... CALL D GENERAL... CALL ADMIRAL D...

He stares. **ADMIZ** looks like a scrambling of letters.

Then it hits him — ADMIZ can be rearranged to **ADMI—Z** ... *ADMIRAL Z?* No, wait. ADMIZ was almost "ADMIRAL" but missing letters.

He writes "ADMIRAL" below and crosses out common letters.

A chill runs through him. There was only one admiral tied to August 1942 who mattered here, August 15th, 1942: *Operation Pedestal.* The convoy that saved Malta. Who do you call? The Admiral. Sir Edward Syfret. He tries **SYFRET** as the passphrase.

The folder clicks open.

Inside, a text file—*ballad.txt*—and a small Python file named *fragment.py*.

He opens *ballad.txt*.

> *Born of iron, Fed by*
> *sea,*
> *My heart broke twice*
> *but never sank.*
> *They lashed me be-*
> *tween my sisters,*
> *And I crawled into*
> *harbour on my knees.*

He closes his eyes for a second because some puzzles are so clean you can taste them. The *Ohio.* Heart broken by bombs, lashed between destroyers, dragged into Grand Harbour, Malta breathes.

He opens *fragment.py*.

```
# fragment.py
Key_fragment = "b4s710n_k3y_p4rt1"
```

A trophy and a test. She is giving him pieces of her fortress for getting this far. He copies the fragment by hand, twice, then kills the folder and scrubs the laptop's memory. He runs three rinse scripts out of habit. Only then does he breathe.

At the window, Valletta winks, on one light at a time, as if the city is deciding, house by house, to continue. He walks out.

His phone buzzes again. Unknown number. He answers, because sometimes you lean into the punch.

"Calaf," a woman says. Liu's voice, clipped, breath controlled like she's speaking while walking past a place she doesn't want to be seen stopping. "Security flagged you. Don't use the guest Wi-Fi at the coworking space; it's a sieve."

"You're watching me now?"

"I'm watching everybody," she says, and hangs up.

He pockets the phone and looks down at the water. Somewhere under those black and blue waves, cables hum with ten thousand lives: salary payments, container bookings, air-con setpoints, alarms that don't go off if their packets get swallowed. He imagines cutting one and listening to the city gasp.

"Trust," Turandot said.

He is not sure who.

He turns back toward the city. The limestone holds the day's heat like memory. He walks fast, then faster, until he feels the old rhythm return—the one that says *you will not sleep, and you will not stop, and you will not lose.*

Tomorrow will be algorithms and ghosts. Tonight is the last quiet.

He is halfway down St. Paul Street when a scooter slides up beside him, engine whine snagging on the walls. The rider lifts his visor—a kid, barely twenty, chin smooth. He holds out a brown envelope.

"For you," the kid says, accent inland Maltese, eyes not unkind. "From a friend."

"Which friend?"

"The kind that pays me to not tell you," the kid says, and is gone, a scream of two-stroke engine and laughter.

His rented flat is a narrow room with a serviceable desk and a balcony over Strait Street.

Inside the envelope: A Polaroid—him at the podium, mid-answer. A red X marked over his chest, hand-drawn and not quite steady. On the back, in neat block letters:

NOBODY SLEEPS TONIGHT.

He huffs a breath that might be a laugh. Nessun Dorma, then. He tucks the photo into his notebook and unlocks the door.

He takes the flash drive Liu gave him from his pocket and holds it against the light. Cheap, generic, unencrypted *until* you try to open it, and then it will bite—she's not careless. He sets it beside the laptop. Not tonight. First rule: don't mix puzzles when you're being watched.

On the balcony, the city feels like a held breath. Somewhere down Strait Street, someone tunes a guitar. A cat decides whether it owns the bonnet of a Peugeot.

His phone buzzes. Unknown number. One line:

> **We saw you with Liu.**
> **She isn't your cover.**
> **She's ours.**

He doesn't reply. He turns off the phone and watches the harbour darken until the cranes are only angles against a sky the colour of hardware.

He turns back to the desk, opens his notebook, and writes three words across a new page:

GATE TWO: TOMORROW.

He underlines **TOMORROW** twice, as if force can make time obedient.

Down on the street, a scooter whines past, the sound catching and receding like a thought. Across the way, a shutter bangs, then stills. The bastions hold their watch. The sea breathes under black glass.

Nobody sleeps tonight.

Morning breaks hard and bright, the kind of Maltese sun that turns limestone into a mirror. Calaf hasn't really slept; the Polaroid with the red X still sits on his desk, a taunt he hasn't decided how to answer.

He slips the flash drive with the riddle his laptop.

Folder opens.

Three files appear:

- *ballad.txt* – the riddle poem

- *fragment.py* – a Python snippet holding a key fragment

- *logfile.dat* – raw diagnostic chatter

He opens *ballad.txt* first.

> *Born of iron,*
> *Fed by sea,*
> *My heart broke twice*
> *but never sank.*
> *They lashed me*
> *between my sisters,*
> *And I crawled*
> *into harbour on my*
> *knees.*

Even on the screen it feels like Malta speaking.

Ohio. There's no other candidate.

He reads it twice to be sure. *Ohio* was the American tanker in Operation Pedestal, lashed between two destroyers, decks awash, still pumping fuel when she limped into Grand Harbour in August 1942. Malta's lifeline.

He opens *fragment.py*.

```
# fragment.py
Key fragment = "b4s710n_k3y_p4rt1"
```

He copies it to his notebook.

Then opens *logfile.dat*. A compressed hex dump, no obvious headers. He decompresses, gets ASCII chatter:

GATEWAY LOG

SIGMA> INIT RND
PROBE

OMEGA>   AUTH
REQ // FRAG ID 1

SIGMA> ACK   .

OMEGA> NEXT?

SIGMA> HOLD

Diagnostic. Not vital — but enough to confirm what he suspected: she's watching every step. Somewhere under Valletta, Turandot is seeing the same log lines. She knows he solved this fast.

He wipes data, powers down, pockets the fragment and goes out.

Outside, the streets smell of left-over rubbish and wet stone. Near St. John's Co-Cathedral, he feels them again — not amateurs. Two men in casual jackets, mirrored spacing: one behind, one on the opposite pavement. Calaf stops to get a pastizzi.

Not police. They'd have stopped him already.

He cuts down Archbishop Street, lengthens stride, doubles through an alley, loops back toward Old Bakery Street. When he reaches his door, there's a white envelope under the mat.

Inside:
STOP OR WE STOP YOU.

He burns it over the sink, watching the flames curl the paper to ash.

He meets Liu at Hastings Gardens, where the bastions give a clean view of Floriana below. She stands by the railing, hair whipped by the wind.

"You tripped a wire," she says before he can speak.

"Better me than you," he says.

"You think they won't connect us? You stood up in front of the entire government yesterday. Everyone in Valletta knows your face now."

"Who?"

"Parliamentary security. Someone flagged your access yesterday. If you go digging again, you'll have company."

Calaf swore under his breath. "Then we need to be faster."

"Faster — and quieter. The last riddle is going to be dangerous, Calaf. If you solve it, the whole treaty falls apart. The government won't forgive that. Neither will Beijing."

There was a pause, then Liu's voice softened.

"Be careful. Turandot may admire your cleverness, but she will still defend her creation — and her father's government — with everything she has."

He hands her the printed poem. "Operation Pedestal. August 1942. The *Ohio*. Confirm me."

She smiles faintly. "My grandfather called her the convoy girl. Said you could smell fuel before you saw her."

Her face goes flat again. "They're taking you seriously now. That note you got? It's the polite version."

"Then I'd better finish before they decide politeness is optional."

"Finish fast," she says. "They've moved me off my usual access. I'm running out of cover."

10 minutes to noon. The MCC hall feels hotter and more charged today. More cameras, more press, more aides

at the front row. Someone has leaked that, "A journalist solved Gate One".

Turandot enters last. Black suit today, hair pinned higher like a crown. She doesn't smile.

"Mr Calaf," she says, voice cutting through the noise. "Have you solved the second riddle?"

He holds up the page. "The answer is the tanker *Ohio*, Operation Pedestal, 15 August 1942."

"Demonstrate," she says.

He walks them through it: ROT13 decoding, anagram of Admiral Syfret's name, convoy date. The hall is rapt — theatre now.

When he finishes, the Bastion logo rotates. Gate Two unlocks with a hollow electronic boom that seems to vibrate in the bones.

Turandot inclines her head. "Correct."

The applause is louder this time. Someone takes a photo. She lets the noise run a moment, then lifts a hand.

"You now hold one fragment of the Bastion key," she says. "Fragments alone are nothing. The third riddle awaits. Are you prepared to solve the last one?"

The screen blanks, then a new symbol flashes: a QR code framed in a topographic map of Grand Harbour.

Before he has a chance to reply, Calaf's phone vibrates: file received. She looks at him.

"Yes."

"Then you have until tomorrow."

The screen flashes.

*If you seek the final
key,
follow the cables.
What lies beneath
will tell you
who you are.*

He cuts across the front row before she can leave. Two aides step forward; she waves them aside.

"Why are you doing this?" he asks quietly.

"Because Malta doesn't have time to wait for accidents to teach her lessons."

"Or because you enjoy watching people dance?"

Something flares in her eyes — not anger, exactly. Curiosity. "Do you think you're dancing?"

"I think you're running a selection program."

"Perhaps," she says. "Perhaps I'm selecting who deserves to hold Malta's future."

"Or who you can trust with it."

That stills her. She studies him for a beat, then says, "Solve the third riddle. Then we'll see if you're right."

He leaves by a side door and heads uphill. Two blocks later, footsteps double behind him. A scooter whines past, rider glancing back.

On Merchants Street, a van idles with its lights off.

He ducks into a church courtyard, waits until the van moves, then doubles back home.

Inside, he locks the door, kills the lights, turns on his laptop and starts on the QR file.

He unpacks the QR file. Compressed archive. Double encryption:

- First layer: key fragment he just obtained.

- Second layer: passphrase.

He brings up a map of Grand Harbour. "*Follow the cables.*" Two landing points near Lascaris Wharf. Beneath them, the Lascaris War Rooms.

He tries "LASCARIS"—denied.

"WARROOMS"—denied.

"UNDERGROUNDOPS" — denied.

Then he remembers her clue: *what lies beneath will tell you who you are.* Not what it's called, but what it *was* — Malta's nerve centre during the siege.

He types: **NERVE** — nothing

He types **LASCARISWHARF** — accepted.

The second layer opens:
BM NI DL QC ZX YH QL HF RT QN IX WZ

Diagraphs, Playfair cipher. But of course.

He sketches a 5×5 grid on his notepad with the keyword LASCARIS, fills in the alphabet, then decrypts digraphs one at a time until the message appears:

TRUSTISKEYDESTROYORHOLD.

He copies it carefully; underlining *TRUST IS KEY. DESTROY OR HOLD* twice.

It's not just a puzzle now. It's a choice.

His phone buzzes. Unknown number, single text:

> **Liu picked up.**
>
> **Parliament security.**
>
> **Holding her Floriana.**
>
> **She hasn't named you.**
>
> **Yet.**

Calaf swears under his breath. He can picture the holding cells — cold stone, damp, designed for intimidation rather than comfort.

He tries calling — no answer.

Hours later, another message:

> **She's dead.**
> **"Suicide."**

He sits very still. Beyond anger now.

He sits very still for a long time. Then he closes the laptop and writes one line across the decrypted page:

Tomorrow: we finish this

He tears out the decrypted page, folds it once, and puts it in his breast pocket.

Tomorrow, he will stand in the hall again.

And he will make her choose.

The Last Gate

The city wakes to a sky the colour of dull nails. Dark clouds above. Valletta's stone glows like an old coin. Calaf stands on his balcony and watches Strait Street rinse itself in pale light: bar shutters rising, a delivery scooter clipping mirrors, a cat making a precise high walk along a gutter like a tightrope. Somewhere, a television blooms open on the morning news, elsewhere radio news in Maltese.

He presses a thumb against the folded paper in his breast pocket as if it might beat. **TRUST IS KEY. DESTROY OR HOLD.** He should rehearse the Playfair steps again—LASCARIS keyed grid, digraphs stepping left and up and across rectangles—but the mathematics isn't the point anymore. The point is that the last gate isn't a gate. It's a cliff.

He locks the door and sits down in front of his desk.

He enters the trophy string from yesterday, the one he wrote twice on paper and nowhere else:

b4s710n_k3y_p4rt1

Accepted. A second prompt blooms, patient, almost polite:

ENTER PASS PHRASE

He whispers the clue one more time, as if the shape of it changes when spoken: "Follow the cables. What lies beneath will tell you who you are."

Lascaris. The war rooms. He types **LAS-CARISWHARF** and taps return.

The archive exhales. A text file opens.

Plain blocks of two-letter gibberish stare back:

BM NI DL QC ZX YH QL HF RT QN IX WZ

There's a temptation to smile — not because it's easy, but because it's honest. An old cipher, precise and stubborn: **Playfair**. You don't brute-force Playfair if it's keyed well; you understand it, one digraph at a time, with a pencil and a willingness to lose an hour getting one letter right.

He pulls the notebook closer, draws again a 5×5 grid, writes the keyword **LASCARIS** across the top, then fills in the rest of the alphabet (I/J combined), left to right, skipping letters already used:

L A S C R
I N B D E
F G H K M
O P Q T U
V W X Y Z

He checks: all letters present, no repeats. The sort of grid a Maltese cryptographer might build at two in the morning with coffee and an argument humming in the next room.

The rules flick through his head like rosary beads:

- Same row: take the letter to the **left** (for decryption).

- Same column: take the letter **above**.

- Rectangle: take letters at the other corners of the rectangle, same row as the original letters, **moving horizontally**.

He starts.

BM: B (row 2, col 3) and M (row 3, col 5).Different row and column — rectangle rule. Opposite corners are **E** (row 2, col 5) and **H** (row 3, col 3).He writes **EH**.

NI: N (row 2, col 2) and I (row 2, col 1).Same row — move left. N –> I, I –> L (wrap). He writes **IL**.

DL: D (row 2, col 4) and L (row 1, col 1).Rectangle: opposite corners **I** (row 2, col 1) and **C** (row 1, col 4). **IC**.

QC: Q (row 4, col 3) and C (row 1, col 4).Rectangle: **T** (row 4, col 4) and **S** (row 1, col 3). **TS**.

ZX: Z (row 5, col 5) and X (row 5, col 3).Same row — move left. Z –> Y, X –> W. **YW**.

YH: Y (row 5, col 4) and H (row 3, col 3).Rectangle: **T** (row 5, col 3) and **K** (row 3, col 4). **TK**.

QL: Q (row 4, col 3) and L (row 1, col 1).Rectangle: **O** (row 4, col 1) and **S** (row 1, col 3). **OS**.

HF: H (row 3, col 3) and F (row 3, col 1).Same row — left. H –> G, F –> V (wrap). **GV**.

RT: R (row 1, col 5) and T (row 4, col 4).Rectangle: **C** (row 1, col 4) and **U** (row 4, col 5). **CU**.

QN: Q (row 4, col 3) and N (row 2, col 2).Rectangle: **P** (row 4, col 2) and **B** (row 2, col 3). **PB**.

IX: I (row 2, col 1) and X (row 5, col 3).Rectangle: **B** (row 2, col 3) and **Y** (row 5, col 1). **BY**.

WZ: W (row 5, col 2) and Z (row 5, col 5).Same row — left. W –> V, Z –> Y. **VY**.

He lines them all up in his notebook:
EH IL IC TS YW TK OS GV CU PB BY VY

He stares at it. Ciphertexts and Playfair grids can be perfidious; sometimes you get the right letters but the wrong keyword order, and you're left squinting at something that looks like a Lithuanian proverb.

He tries natural language recombination, writes it as a stream:
EHILICTSYWTKOSGVCUPBBYVY

Then he sees it — not the letters themselves, but the cadence of how Turandot writes when she sharpens a point. He spaces differently:
TRUST IS KEY DESTROY OR HOLD

Because of course she'd pick a grid, a key, a rule set to say a thing she can't quite bring herself to say aloud: that at the end of all your locks and cleverness, the final gate is never math. It's **trust**.

He writes the sentence clean across a fresh page, as if making vows:

TRUST IS KEY. DESTROY OR HOLD.

He takes a photo of the notebook, prints it on the small thermal printer he keeps for bad exits and worse interviews, then burns the paper grid in a bowl and flushes the ash.

When he looks up, daylight is pushing at the blinds. On the street below, a bin lorry moans; a cat debates whether to own the bonnet of a Peugeot.

His phone buzzes. Unknown number. A single line:

> **Floriana cell empty.**
> **Liu gone.**
> **"Suicide."**

He closes his eyes. There's a point past which grief is not a thing you feel, but a tool you pick up — edge toward, edge away from, knowing you'll need it held steady when you put it to work. He closes his eyes. Beyond anger now — the message is a tool.

He grabs his coat and the notebook and goes to end the game.

The watchers are tidier today. He spots only one for sure—navy jacket, the posture of someone paid to forget he has a spine. The van that used to idle with its lights off now idles with them *on*, a promise and a dare. Fine. Let them walk him to the MCC like state-provided company.

On Republic Street, the protestors are back. Their signs bloom like weeds: **NO SECRET ANNEX**, **WE ARE NOT A CORRIDOR**, **BURN THE BASTION** scrawled with uneven fury, **SAVE THE BASTION** painted with neat disgust. A man with a megaphone quotes the constitution. A woman with a face with sharp edges and a few scars stares a police line into reconsidering its life choices. The city smells of coffee and fear.

At the Mediterranean Conference Centre, the foyer is already full. The air hums with rehearsal: aides practicing phrases into phones—*operational continuity, strategic patience, temporary suspension*. A television crew runs a light meter across Turandot's empty podium and nods, satisfied with the luminosity of the absence.

Debrincat stands near the sponsor wall, shirt perfect, smile serrated. He looks like a man in the last five minutes of a game he intends to win by flipping the table.

"Mr Calaf," he says as Calaf passes, as if the words taste of something he can't quite spit out. "Enjoying your time as a performer?"

"Not a performer," Calaf says. "A witness."

"Is that what you call it when you help set fire to your host's house?"

"Better than selling it," Calaf says, and keeps walking.

Debrincat's smile thins to a thread. "You don't know this island," he murmurs to Calaf's shoulder. "You confuse stubbornness with sovereignty."

Calaf doesn't turn. "Sometimes they're the same word."

He takes his place at the aisle, back to the wall. Old habits are stubborn for a reason.

The hall fills with the careful sound of important people each making sure they're seen. Chairs scrape. Badges glint. Another blond watcher in navy enters late and takes a seat that is not a seat so much as a declaration of proximity to whatever will happen.

Then Turandot arrives.

No introduction. No warm-up act. She steps onto the stage as though she has just climbed one more stone stair and found the next level of the fortress. Charcoal suit. Hair pinned high like order. Her face is not indifferent. It is intent.

She presses her fingertips to the podium, and the hall stills without being asked.

"In a siege," she says, "you ration everything—food, water, ammunition, courage. You ration trust most of all."

Silence. Even the ambitious stop checking their reflections in their phones.

"The Bastion Protocol is our rationing plan for catastrophe," she continues. "It is also—by design and by necessity—a gatekeeper. I set three gates to be sure that anyone who reached the heart of the system had earned their way there. Mr Calaf reached the third."

A day ago, that might have sounded like a sneer. Today it sounds like the naming of a fact in a ledger.

She lifts her gaze to the aisle where Calaf stands. It lands on him and holds, the way a surveyor sets a point and measures the world from it. "Mr Calaf," she says. "Have you solved the third gate?"

He touches the paper in his pocket and hears the echo of the ciphertext like a distant machine. "Yes."

"Deliver."

His footsteps tilt the room's axis as he moves down the aisle. The side mic is ten paces into bright light, the sort that makes men look brave or foolish. The microphone smells faintly of new plastic and someone else's nervous breath.

He unfolds the strip of paper (the habit of a man who refuses to let silicon have all the memory) and reads aloud:

"Trust is key. Destroy or hold."

There is no murmuring now. The sound that goes through the room is heavier than that—an animal shifting in sleep.

Turandot doesn't look away from him. "Your method," she says, because the ritual matters. It's not the answer on the paper; it's the path to it.

"Playfair cipher," he says. "Keyword LASCARIS. Grid built left to right with I/J combined. Decrypt each digraph—left for same row, up for same column, rectangle swap for the rest. It gives the line as written."

A few heads nod—the engineers, the old men who remember when Malta was run on pencils and stubbornness. In the front row, a young aide looks from one to the other as if hoping someone will pass out a multiple-choice quiz.

Turandot lifts her hand. The big screen behind her wakes: the Bastion console, serene as a chapel, with three vertical pillars of light. Two are dark; one pulses pale, waiting. You could mistake it for a hospital monitor or an electrocardiogram. You would not be wrong.

"You now possess the final semantic key," she says. "The Bastion will accept a command in two parts: the **what** and the **who**. The **what** is the option before us. The **who** is the voice with the authority to speak it."

Debrincat stands so fast his chair complains. "The Prime Minister expects the Bastion to remain live pending the treaty signing," he says, voice smooth and edged with a threat he thinks reads as patience. "We will not sabotage a national asset on the basis of a—of a theatrical exercise."

Turandot doesn't even turn. "This is not theatre, Mr Debrincat," she says, and it is not a correction so much as a small change in gravity. "This is an audit."

"We are hours from a signing. Beijing expects—"

"Beijing does not govern Malta," she says. "Nor does Brussels. Nor do you."

A ripple moves through the room like a gust. Debrincat's mouth smiles; his eyes don't.

"Your remit—" he begins.

"My remit," she says, "is to defend the island. Not the government of the day. If those two diverge, the duty is to the island."

She steps down from the podium. The aides quiver like a school of fish tracking a predator's shadow. She stops a few feet from Calaf, within range of the sound of his breath, and lowers her voice so that the microphones pick it up and the room has to lean in to hear.

"You asked me why riddles," she says. "Because Malta learns by siege. Because I needed to know if someone could meet me at the gate and still ask for the right thing."

"What's the right thing?" he asks, though he knows.

She steps closer.

"The thing that doesn't let Liu die for nothing. She told me about the Annexe B, the secret backdoor agreement and the money involved. Without her I wouldn't have known."

Her mouth moves around the name like a cut you can't keep from touching.

He nods. The kind of nod that is a pact.

"Then destroy it," he says. "With me watching."

She doesn't flinch. The flinch happened last night, somewhere only she saw. She turns back to the console.

She places her hand on the scanner. The machine takes what it needs from a body to know it is the right one: palm print, vein, heat, the cadence of a heartbeat. It accepts.

Authorise identity.
Her voice is steady. "Turandot Vassallo."

Command?
She breathes in. She breathes out. "**Destroy.**"

The console is a polite executioner. It asks without malice: **Confirm.**

Turandot's eyes find Calaf's. "Together," she says.

"Confirm," he says, though the machine doesn't require him for anything except the geometry of responsibility. Sometimes witness is function.

She enters a string—long, ungainly, the sort of thing only the person who wrote it would bother to memorise. Her hands don't shake.

Bastion Core Erasure Protocol v1.4 — INIT
Everything after that is mechanical:

- **Wiping HSM shards ... OK**

- **Rotating KMS salts ... OK**

- **Dismantling threshold signatures ... OK**

- **Overwriting failover maps ... OK**

- **Burning cold backups ... OK**

- **Shredding audit trails ... OK**

- **Self-destruct heartbeat ... ARMED**

The progress bar creeps toward an end that will feel like a drop. The room has stopped breathing.

Debrincat shouts to cut the feed. No one moves. The AV obeys whoever designed it to obey the transparent act. Today, that's her.

The bar hits 100%. The three pillars turn grey. The console lines render one last answer like a priest closing a book.

**BASTION PRO-
TOCOL**

—

DESTROYED

NO   RECOVERY
POSSIBLE

Silence.

Not just quiet—the particular silence that arrives after a blow finally lands.

Somewhere behind them a phone begins to vibrate, then another, then a chorus. A junior aide makes a helpless sound that might be the beginning of a prayer. The blond watcher closes his eyes once, opens them again, and doesn't look surprised.

Turandot removes her hand from the console as if she is letting go of someone's pulse. She doesn't look triumphant. She looks like a person who has finally done the thing she could not not do.

She turns to Calaf. "Now we live with it."

He nods. He has no line big enough for this.

The room remembers it contains people with jobs and starts to shatter into motion. Debrincat is already halfway to the side door, phone to his ear, smile back on like armour, voice sugared and lethal. "Of course, Prime Minister. No, we will control the narrative. Yes. She acted—yes. I understand."

Calaf steps into the aisle. The hall tilts into chaos: journalists break formation like birds, microphones tilt and weave, cameras stumble into their operators' shoulders. A woman from a foreign outlet is already practicing her live stand-up, voice pitched to a sympathetic hysteria: *In an unprecedented... the Prime Minister is expected... sources tell us the Chinese delegation...*

He leaves the hall by the side staircase, the way a man leaves a church after the wedding when he is not family and does not need to perform grief or relief. Turandot falls in beside him without asking. Two security guards fall behind them at a distance that says, *We are paid to care about your skull but not your soul.*

In the stairwell, a guy steps out of a shadow, hands visible, weight on his heels like a man trying to stand on a boat.

"Bravu," he says softly to Turandot, the Maltese vowel like a stone landing in a still pool. Not mockery. Assessment. He looks at Calaf and gives the smallest nod, the kind men who have played on opposite teams give one another when someone lands a clean shot. Then he steps aside.

Outside, Valletta is bright and hard. The air smells of concrete dust and salt. A gull shrieks like something being cut.

They walk down toward the Fort St Elmo because of course they do; when you blow a hole in a fortress, you go to look what is still standing.

On the way down, Calaf's phone buzzes. He glances:
UNKNOWN — MGARR. He answers.

Timur's voice is weather and knives. "You've done it,
then."

"We've done it," Calaf says, glancing at Turandot.

Timur is silent long enough to be a question. Then:
"Russians in the marina. Chinese in the cafés. Brussels at
the Phoenicia bar pretending they don't drink whisky at
noon. You've set the table. Everyone's hungry."

"Advice?"

"Remember that applause isn't cover," Timur says.
"And listen for the people who lost something real. They'll
tell you where the bodies will be buried next." The line
clicks dead. He has always been generous with love and
miserly with permission to fail.

They reach the rail. The Grand Harbour lies spread out
like a diagram: cranes drawing arcs, ferries stitching silver
threads that unspool and vanish, bastions hemming water
like careful handwriting. The air has the taste it gets before
rain, metallic and clean.

"Liu," Turandot says without preface. The name falls
and makes a circle in the air that neither of them speaks
into.

"They'll call it suicide," Calaf says.

"They like the word because it erases verbs," she says. "It
lets them say *it happened* instead of *someone did it*."

They stand a long time without speaking. Two tourists drift near, feel the weather in the air around these strangers, and drift away again, offended by something they cannot name.

"This will cost us," Turandot says at last. "Funding. Leverage. Confidence. People who believed in the Bastion will feel betrayed."

"They're allowed," Calaf says. "But the price of holding it would have been far worse. They just wouldn't have seen the bill until later. The endless possibilities for corruption."

She glances at him. "You're going to publish."

"I am."

She waits for him to apologise for it. He does not.

"Do it clean," she says finally.

"I intend to."

"And if I ask you a question you won't like?" he says.

She lifts an eyebrow. *Try me.*

"Was there a version where you held?"

She looks back at the harbour. The cranes keep their patient arcs. When she speaks it is quieter than the wind. "If Liu had lived," she says, "I would have told myself there was time. That we could hold until the politics were safer. That money and who is receiving it and where it went doesn't matter. That we could keep the lock without selling the door. That is the lie that breaks small countries."

He nods. He doesn't touch her. Not now.

A siren starts somewhere on the other side and moves across the city like a zipper being slowly undone. The sky finally commits to rain—thin at first, then thicker, as if the island has decided to wash its face.

They turn back toward the city. Her security guards give them umbrellas.

By the time they reach the MCC up the street, the news has already begun to write itself without their help. A vendor's radio spits headlines like sparks: "—Prime Minister under pressure—" "—opposition demands emergency session—" "—Chinese embassy requests—" "—EU to convene—".

At the MCC's side entrance, the press has crystallised into formation. Microphones tilt like a field of hostile flowers.

A man with a blindingly white smile calls, "Ms Vassallo, did you just topple the government?"

Another: "Mr Calaf, are you coordinating with Brussels?"

A woman shouts: "Is this an act of cyber-terrorism?"

Turandot closes her umbrella, walks straight through the noise without increasing her speed. The guards open a path. Calaf follows. Someone's shoulder clips his; he smells sweat and fear. Someone else hisses *traitor* in Maltese and then looks surprised at his own courage.

Inside, the building exhales air-conditioner breath. The atrium is a heat sink for panic: people running in lines that almost resemble purpose. A junior minister is practicing blame in a reflective panel. A civil servant with a helmet of hair is on her fifth coffee and her first smile.

In a small conference room with a glass wall and blinds drawn halfway, Turandot sits, draws a deep breath, and rests her forehead briefly against the heel of her hand. Not a gesture of defeat. Calibration. She drops her hand and is composed again before the blinds stop swaying.

Calaf sets his notebook on the table and turns on a small recorder. He doesn't make the mistake of being coy about it. She notices, nods.

"On record," she says.

He asks clean questions. She answers cleanly: her design intent, the gates, the reason for public tests. The pressure from Debrincat, the timing of the treaty. She does not speculate about Liu; she uses the kind of nouns that can be admitted into evidence. Annexe B content. The backdoor agreement.

At the end she says, "There will be other Bastions. Built by people less interested in transparency and more in control."

"Then we keep solving riddles," he says.

A corner of her mouth lifts—something that could almost be a smile in a life which afforded that luxury. "Next time," she says, "you bring the first one."

A knock at the door. A woman with a lanyard and a voice like a metronome: "Press conference in five. Then Parliament."

Turandot rises. "You will write," she says to Calaf. Not a request. An expectation. "Do it clean."

"Do it public," he says.

"I just did," she says, and is gone.

Calaf stands a moment in the quiet that follows people who do not waste their time or yours. He looks at the recorder. The little red light blinks a patient beat. He switches it off.

He walks back into the atrium, into the rushing weather of the day. The broadcast screens bloom headlines faster than you could type them if you still used ten fingers: **BASTION DESTROYED**; **PM UNDER FIRE**; **CHINA DEMANDS EXPLANATION**; **EU PRAISES TRANSPARENCY, SEEKS DETAILS**. The words move as if the world is deciding what has already happened.

By evening, Parliament convenes an emergency session. Calaf watches from the press gallery as men in suits arrange their faces into expressions of concern. The Prime Minister speaks without saying anything that could be construed as a sentence in history; he is a man trying to walk on coals while his shoes are already on fire. The opposition leader speaks with the satisfied anger of a man who can smell promotion. A back-bench MP, her hair yanked into a bun of moral certainty, calls for an inquiry with teeth. Debrincat sits very still, hands folded, mouth set at a degree that will be read as scorekeeping.

Before the late news, the Prime Minister resigns live. He utters words that amount to *I will not be the person you say I am* and leaves the podium by a door that wasn't there yesterday. The anchor blinks, recalibrates, and looks grateful to have been given history instead of having to make it.

Calaf walks to his flat through streets that hum like a field full of bees. People are both louder and quieter than usual. Bars turn their televisions toward the glass so the street can see. A woman cries softly into her phone outside a pharmacy. A boy skateboards down a handrail with the concentration of someone who believes that if he lands this one, the island will right itself.

In his flat, he sits at the desk and opens a new document. The words come clean, unadorned. He learned a long time ago that the sentences you can stand by in a courtroom are the only sentences worth writing on days like this.

Inside the Bastion: The Day Malta Chose the Gate.

He writes past midnight. He stops once when he finds himself typing word heroic, he thinks a bit and then deletes it. He writes word choice instead. Better.

He encrypts the file and sends it to three places that he would be embarrassed to admit he trusts. He prints one hard copy, tucking it into the lining of his bag the way people used to conceal cash at borders.

There is a soft knock.

He goes to the door with his weight set right. Turandot stands on the threshold, coat damp, hair pulled back in a way that tells the truth about the day's length.

"You came," he says.

"You asked me to go on record," she says. "Best to do it before someone decides I shouldn't."

He steps aside. She enters. He sets the recorder between them like a small, honest animal and presses the button. She gives him one clean page: the gates, the console, the sentence she whispered to herself before she said "Destroy." She does not ask to take anything back. He does not offer.

He clicks off the recorder. For a second, no one breathes.

"What now?" he asks.

"There will be other bastions," she says. "Other treaties. Other riddles."

"Then we keep solving."

She almost smiles. "Next time, you bring the first one." She's already said it, but some lines are true enough to be worth saying twice.

She leaves. He locks the door. He sits in the quiet that follows a good day and a bad day that happen to be the same day.

His phone buzzes. Gozo. Timur:

> **New players landing.**
>
> **Don't mistake applause for cover.**
>
> **Proud of you.**
>
> **Sleep.**

He turns off the lights.

Outside, Valletta is a map that breathes. Under the water, the cables hum like arteries. The fortress is gone.

The gates are not.

Epilogue

Within hours, Valletta is a furnace. Prime Minister resigns live on television. Parliament convenes an emergency session. Opposition smells blood.

The next morning, the caretaker government is sworn in — its first act is to suspend the treaty and announce a full inquiry into the Bastion Protocol.

Across the world, headlines roar:

- **Times of Malta:** *Bastion Protocol Destroyed — PM Resigns Amid Crisis*

- **The Guardian:** *Malta Blows Up Its Own Cyber Shield as China Deal Collapses*

- **Financial Times:** *EU Races to Secure Mediterranean Data Corridor After Bastion Wipe*

- **South China Morning Post:** *Beijing 'Gravely Concerned' After Malta's Sudden Withdrawal from Pact*

- **New York Times:** *Tiny Malta Sparks Global*

Cybersecurity Debate

- **Politico EU:** *Valletta Moves First: EU Now Faces Data Sovereignty Reckoning*

- **Al Jazeera:** *Malta's Digital Uprising: A Small Nation's Defiance Goes Viral*

Outside the Parliament, Republic Street fills with both cheers and fury. **TURANDOT FOR PRESIDENT** banners clash with chants of **YOU'VE MADE US A TARGET.** At cafés, pensioners argue. In bars, bartenders mutter about servers going down.

Valletta feels like a city holding its breath.

Three weeks later, the caretaker government is still barely standing, Brussels inspectors hover, Parliament's inquiry is must-watch television.

Calaf leans on his balcony. Below, duelling graffiti:

**TURANDOT   =
HERO**

**SHE   SOLD   US
OUT**

On TV, pundits shout about sovereignty, surveillance, and whether Malta has doomed itself or saved its soul.

His phone buzzes — a warning from Timur:

> **Russians at Mgarr.**
>
> **Chinese still circling.**
>
> **Bastion gone but cables remain.**
>
> **Careful, son.**
>
> **You've made yourself visible again.**

A knock. Turandot stands there, rain on her coat.

"You're leaving," she says.

"Story's filed," he says. "But Malta will be talking about you for a long time."

"They already are. Half want a statue. Half want me in handcuffs. Next time," she says, "the riddles won't be mine."

"Then I'll be ready."

She almost smiles — almost — then turns and vanishes down the stairwell, leaving only the echo of her footsteps.

Calaf stubs out the cigarette, goes back to the desk.

Beyond the window, Valletta argues about the future; below, Turandot's figure disappears into the rain-slicked street — and inside, Calaf begins to write the one story that might decide it.

THE END

Author's Note – Cryptography

D id you ever write secret messages in school? I did. Secret codes, transposed words. I've always been fascinated by cryptography. Cryptology or cryptography has been used since the time of Romans and likely before that too. When military or spies were involved, information had to be kept secret. I used the internet and other sources for the cryptography in this story.

The riddles in this story are built on real cryptographic methods — ones that you could solve with pencil, paper, and a little persistence.

Using these real ciphers ties the story to Malta's history as a centre of Allied codebreaking in WWII (the Lascaris War Rooms under Valletta were the actual plotting centre for the Mediterranean theatre). The solutions Calaf provides are based on history, Dingli cliffs had a wireless intercept station. Operation Pedestal and the arrival of S/S Ohio battered as it was and nearly sinking before its arrival at the Grand Harbour, was a true lifesaver to Malta. Malta had been bombed more than London, and by August 15,

1942, Malta was starving. The convoy became known as the *Santa Marija Convoy*.

It also shows that the "game" Turandot has built isn't random — it rewards thinking, pattern recognition, and persistence, just like real cryptography challenges do.

If you enjoyed the riddles in this story and want to know more about how the riddles were solved, read on. The following explains the real cryptographic methods used — and includes a challenge you can solve yourself, with a worked-out solution at the end if you would like to check your work.

ROT13 – The Simple Substitution

ROT13 ("rotate by 13") is one of the simplest ciphers ever used.It replaces each letter with the one 13 places later in the alphabet (wrapping around at Z).Because the English alphabet has 26 letters, ROT13 is its own reverse — applying it twice gets you back to the original text.

Example:

NQZVA → ADMIZ

PNYY → CALL

QRARENY → DGENERAL

This is easy to decode — but that's the point. Turandot uses it as a *warm-up layer*, a gate that lets the cleverest challengers through to the real puzzle.

Playfair Cipher – The Wartime Puzzle

The Playfair cipher is a classical encryption method developed in the 1850s by Charles Wheatstone and promoted by Lord Playfair. It was widely used by the British military during WWI and WWII for field messages because it could be solved and transmitted quickly without machines.

It works like this:

1. **Create a 5×5 grid** of letters using a secret keyword (e.g., LASCARIS).

   - Fill in the keyword first (omitting duplicate letters), then the remaining letters of the alphabet in order (combining I/J).

2. **Break the message into pairs of letters** (digraphs).

3. **Decrypt each pair** using three simple rules:

   - **Same row:** replace each with the letter to the *left* (for decryption).

- ○ **Same column:** replace each with the letter *above*.

- ○ **Rectangle:** take the letters at the opposite corners of the rectangle.

Playfair is much more secure than ROT13, but still solvable by hand — exactly the sort of puzzle Calaf, as a trained intelligence analyst, would tackle under pressure.

Reader Challenge

ROT13: shifts each letter 13 places; trivial, but satisfying to strip away.

Playfair Cipher: used in WWI & WWII. Build a 5×5 grid from a keyword, decrypt digraphs with left/above/rectangle rules.

Riddle:

> *Once a bulwark, now*
> *a memory,   I*
> *stood when the Cres-*
> *cent stormed the sea.*
> *They called me victori-*
> *ous,   though my name*

was small, Three cities
I guard, one city I be-
came.

Answer: **BIRGU** (also called Vittoriosa, the Victorious one) stronghold during the Great Siege of 1565. It's one of the Tri-Cities on the south side of the Grand Harbour. Birgu also has the Fort Saint Angelo which was instrumental in the defence against the Ottoman Empire. Use as keyword, then decrypt this ciphertext:

HE NQ EO OF LF QY

Hint: The plaintext is two words you can imagine shouted from the bastions.

Solution – Spoiler Alert!

Keyword: BIRGU → build the grid by writing B I R G U, then the remaining letters A–Z (skipping J and duplicates):

B I R G U
A C D E F
H K L M N
O P Q S T
V W X Y Z

Decrypt the pairs using the rules above. You'll get:
MALTASTANDSX
Drop the padding **X → MALTA STANDS**.
(*Why the X?* Playfair often inserts an X to split double letters or pad the final pair.)

BASTION BUTTERFLY

One promise. One prayer.

And a butterfly too fragile to survive the war.

A.K. LAKELETT

Faukon Abbey Publishing

Contents

BASTION BUTTERFLY

ONE PROMISE. ONE PRAYER. AND A BUTTERFLY TOO FRAGILE TO SURVIVE THE WAR.

BOOK 3 IN BASTION TRILOGY

A.K.LAKELETT

Prologue
Sliema, 1984.

The morning sun glanced off the sea and into the kitchen window where Joseph sits with his birthday coffee. He is forty today, trim from morning swims, his hair just beginning to silver at the temples. Across the table, his wife places a wrapped parcel beside his toast. Their eight-year-old son leans forward, curious.

"This came by hand," she says. "An older woman, who gave her name as Carmen, delivered it."

Joseph frowns, intrigued. Every year of his life he had received a birthday gift—always a butterfly. He never knew who sent them. First drawings, then crochet, later delicate Maltese lace. He has kept them all, placed them inside frames. They were beautiful. But this paper package was heavier, more like a book.

He unties the string carefully. Inside lays a slim, leather-bound diary and a single note in a shaky hand:

She wanted you to have this when she could no longer send butterflies.

Joseph runs his thumb over the cover. The leather feels soft, worn, smooth. He glances at his son, then opens to the first page, there is a butterfly of white Maltese lace —

the most beautiful yet. He lifts it up, and places it on the table. On the page he sees a careful, flowing script.

The harbour smelled of smoke and oranges tonight, and I write this by lamplight with ink that keeps blotting in the damp. On the 14th of April, 1943, I met a man who changed my life —

The Dance in Valletta

The searchlights swept over Valletta's Grand Harbour, their thin beams briefly catching the sheen of the anchored ships before disappearing into the low clouds. It was April, and the evenings were still cool. The breeze coming off the sea carried a faint bite. Somewhere across the water a siren wailed once, then fell silent. The Maltese capital was used to these nights—blackout curtains, muffled lamps, streets empty except for the tramp of boots or the growl of army trucks. In the Lascaris War Rooms, buried under the bastions, the night shift continued to tick away in pencil and Morse code. Maria Bonnici pulled her cardigan closer around her shoulders as she put down her pencil and straightened from the plotting desk.

Maria was seventeen, a slip of a girl with serious brown eyes and hair that always escaped the pins she tried to hold it down with. She was proud of this job, proud to be doing her bit for the war, even if it meant long hours underground and late walks home through the deserted streets. Her mother worried. Respectable Valletta families did not send their daughter out after dark, with all those unruly military men about. But her father had said, "Let the girl serve. We need every pair of hands."

Maria Bonnici bent over her logbook, recording the movements of aircraft reported by radar and visual spotters. She'd been underground for hours. Filling pages with her neat handwriting, recording aircraft movements in the dimly lit War Rooms. The shift had been quiet—just a handful of reconnaissance flights to record—but the stillness always left her tense, waiting for the sudden rush of sirens.

Although she was a civilian, her job was vital—everything plotted here would go upstairs to the plotting table that controlled Malta's anti-aircraft guns. No raids, only reconnaissance flights.

She glanced at the clock—ten minutes to nine—and reached for the mug of tea by her elbow. The night smelled faintly of damp limestone, sweat, and the tang of kerosene from the lamps. Somewhere further down the tunnel, a group of British WAAFs giggled, then fell silent at the sharp rebuke of a sergeant.

"Bonnici?" Sergeant Camilleri appeared at the doorway to the plotting room, his cap pushed back. "Your relief is here. Go on, go home, get some fresh air."

Maria nodded gratefully. She signed off in the log, hung her headphones carefully on their hook, and left the room. The long corridor felt endless after the cramped plotting table, and her footsteps echoed softly on the stone. It was warm under-ground; the sudden freshness of the night air made her shiver. At the end of the tunnel, she climbed the shallow steps that led out behind the bastions.

The night air was damp and chilly, and she shivered as she set off along the narrow path toward the nearest gate. Valletta was trying to fall into a restless sleep under curfew and blackout, the only sounds being the distant lap of water and the occasional rattle of a truck on the cobbles, the narrow streets lit only by the sliver of moon above. Somewhere, a gramophone was playing faint swing music, a tune carried by the night breeze.

"Farfetta! Farfetta! *Stenna*! Wait!"

Maria turned at the sound of Carmen's voice floating from the door leading down the long limestone corridor that ran from the Lascaris War Rooms to the open air. A sudden flash of light before the door closed, then the passage fell back into shadow. Carmen jogged the last few yards, cardigan slipping from one shoulder, cheeks flushed.

"You'll miss the curfew if you dawdle," she called in Maltese, looping her arm through Maria's. "*Tridx tinqabad fil-kesħa*—don't get caught in the cold."

"It has already found me," Maria said, smiling despite the ache between her shoulders. Hours bent over the plotting table left a thin pain there, like a string pulled too tight.

They climbed the shallow steps and came out behind the bastions. The April moon hid behind the clouds; darkness lay over Grand Harbour, ships becoming dark cut-outs on the water until the moon shone on the sea again. The breeze smelled of salt and diesel and the faint sweetness of orange blossom. Even in the midst of war, some orange trees were still growing somewhere between the streets. Maria breathed in the fresh sea air to get rid of the mustiness of the underground out of her lungs.

Ahead, two men in khaki stood with their backs to the view. At the sound of the girls' footsteps, they turned. One wore his cap at a rakish angle and grinned as though meeting an old friend.

"Evening, ladies," he said, clearly American. "Didn't mean to startle you."

Maria slowed, wary, but curious. The taller of the two men grinned as he stepped closer, the lamplight catching on the polished buttons of his U.S. Navy uniform.

Carmen slowed, taking stock. "Il-lejl it-tajjeb," she answered, adding in English, "Good evening."

The grinning one tipped his cap. "Lieutenant Benjamin Franklin Pinkerton. Call me Ben, at your service." Tall, broad-shouldered, and he wore a freshly pressed khaki uniform that marked him as U.S. Navy. The other man, a little shorter and older looking, gave her an apologetic smile and nodded politely. "Charlie Mason. We're just off the ship. Looking for the right way back to the main square." Charlie's smile was faint but genuine. "Ma'am," he said, and then, with a careful little bow that looked learned rather than natural, "*signorinas*."

Maria glanced at the heavy door behind them. "You're lost. This way is not for the public."

Maria's first instinct was to be cautious. American servicemen were common enough these days—Malta was filling up with troops for the coming invasion—but she had been raised to be wary of strange men. Her mother's voice echoed in her head, warning about foreign soldiers—but there was nothing threatening in Charlie's quiet manner. Pinkerton, though, was grinning at her as if she were the first girl he had seen in months.

Pinkerton laughed softly. "We followed our noses to the view. It's something, isn't it?" He tipped his head toward the black sweep of harbour. "Do you work down there?"

"Yes," she said simply.

"That must be where the island's brain lives." His tone was teasing, but his curiosity was real. "Seems to me we owe you a drink."

"It's late," Carmen said before Maria could answer. "Curfew is nearly here."

"Then let us walk you," Pinkerton offered easily tipping his cap. "You never know what kind of characters are out on these streets." His tone made it clear he thought he was the only character they needed to worry about.

It was awkward to refuse an officer without seeming rude. Charlie's quiet steadiness softened the boldness of the other man. Carmen and Maria looked at each other and nodded. They set off four abreast along the narrow lanes. Their footsteps rang on stone; a winch squealed and clanked in the docks below. The searchlights were idle tonight, their pale spears resting against low clouds.

Pinkerton kept the cold at bay with words. He told them about their convoy from Algiers, about coffee aboard ship that pretended to be American, about a near miss with a mine that he turned into a joke. He had a way of making ordinary things perform for him. Maria, who had meant to keep silent, found herself answering politely, her fingers curled into her cardigan against the chill.

At Strada Reale they stopped. Shops were shuttered; the street was a tunnel of dark.

"My house is this way," Maria said. A small nod of farewell.

Pinkerton tipped his cap. "Anytime. Perhaps we'll see you again, Miss—"

"Bonnici," Carmen supplied. "Farfetta, curfew."

Pinkerton cocked his head. "Farfetta?"

Carmen laughed. "Her nickname from school."

"Sounds like farfalle," he said, delighted. "Pasta."

Maria's cheeks warmed. "I am not pasta," she said, half-scandalised, half-amused.

"It means butterfly," Carmen told him, eyes dancing. "She played one in a school play. The wings were too big, and she knocked over a plant, and Sister Bernadette shouted so loud the whole parish heard."

Pinkerton's grin widened. "A butterfly behind a bastion. I like that."

Maria pretended not to like that he liked it. "*Il-lejl it-taj-jeb*—good night," she said, firmer than she felt and turned quickly, and hurried away before her blush betrayed her.

Two evenings later, when Maria and Carmen came up the corridor into the damp air, Pinkerton and Charlie were waiting near the gate with two sweating bottles of Coca--Cola.

"Imported delicacy," Pinkerton announced. "Don't tell the black market I undercut them."

Carmen raised an eyebrow. "We prefer tea with shame," she said impishly.

"What's tea with shame?" Charlie asked, amused.

"Tea with nothing to put in it," Carmen said. "Because there is nothing."

Pinkerton laughed, then sobered. "You can't keep walking home alone. Let us take you somewhere better. There's a dance on tonight, over in Floriana. The band is playing real music. Come with us. What do you say?"

Maria hesitated. The idea of dancing with an American sailor in a public hall made her stomach flutter. But it was cold, and the thought of music and warmth was tempting. She had never been to a dance. Her mother would not approve. But the thought of music, of an evening not spent in the blackout gloom, tempted her.

"I don't know how."

Pinkerton's grin widened. "Then I'll teach you.."

The hall in Floriana was warm enough to fog the windows. Candles guttered in saucers along the walls. And so, for the first time, Maria Bonnici found herself in a dance hall filled with GIs and sailors. The hall was warm and crowded, the band playing swing music that made the floor shake and laughter rise over the blackout curtains. A sergeant's wife played piano with determined cheer; a corporal sawed at a fiddle; an improvised drum kit thumped like a second heartbeat. Someone said the tune was Glenn Miller "as remembered by a Maltese cousin."

Pinkerton bowed extravagantly. "Miss Bonnici, may I?"

He led her in slow counted steps, his hand at the respectful part of her back, his other holding hers lightly. "One-two, one-two-three." He didn't show off at first. When he did, he telegraphed every turn so she could follow and finish laughing, rather than sprawled on the floor.

Across the room, Carmen danced with Charlie. He moved like a man who'd rather watch than be watched, content to let Carmen laugh for both of them.

"Again?" Pinkerton asked eagerly.

Maria surprised herself. "Again." Pinkerton swept her into a jitterbug, spinning her until she was dizzy and laughing despite herself. For a little while she forgot the war, forgot the chilly streets and the silent plotting tables, and let herself be a girl at a dance.

They danced until the windows ran with steam and somebody propped the door open for air. Maria's hairpins surrendered; she did not care. For the first time in weeks, she laughed without counting the laughs. When the band finally slowed into a foxtrot, Pinkerton adjusted easily, keeping her balanced as if he had decided that was his job. When the tune ended, Charlie fetched water for the four of them and made sure no one pressed too close to the girls.

Outside, the wind cut through sweat-damp dresses. Pinkerton shifted automatically to Maria's windward side, blocking the worst of it. It was a small thing, but she noticed.

"You should let me see you again," he said. "There aren't many good things in this war, Farfetta. But you might just be one of them."

Maria blushed and nodded, not trusting her voice.

"You are very forward," she said, as they walked back toward Valletta afterward. Carmen and Charlie followed behind them.

"Life's too short not to be," he said cheerfully. "You never know when Jerry's going to drop something on our heads. You've got to grab what happiness you can."

"Do you miss home?" he asked quietly as they walked.

"Home is here," she said.

"I meant before the war. Before the underground rooms and the pencils."

She thought of summer feasts, fireworks spilling stars over church domes, her brothers pinwheeling down Strada Reale. "Sometimes," she said.

He nodded. "Me too. There's a diner in Chicago that does pancakes at midnight. Before the war, I thought that was important." He smiled, almost to himself. "Now I think warm socks are important."

"Warm socks are very important," Maria agreed gravely, and they both laughed.

At her door, he repeated his request to see her again. Maria hesitated, then nodded. "But not too late," she said. "I have to work."

"Not too late," he promised.

Days grew a little longer. The island's pace quickened—more lorries, more uniforms, a sense that something was coming. Pinkerton and Charlie appeared as if conjured whenever Maria's shift ended, waiting to walk her home or take her for a stroll on the bastion walls when she had an afternoon free. Pinkerton made her laugh, brought her sweets, and tinned peaches. Sometimes Carmen came; sometimes her mother kept her home to mind a nephew. They walked on the bastions, looking out over the dark harbour lit by searchlights. They shared sandwiches under the stars. Slowly, Maria found herself looking forward to his grin, to the way he made her laugh. Charlie was always there too. He didn't say much, revealing only a little about himself. He was a quiet presence who made sure Pinkerton got her home before curfew.

Pinkerton talked about everything and nothing: the ridiculousness of naval forms, a baseball team that did not exist anymore because the boys had all joined up. He told stories to make her laugh.

Charlie, when he spoke, asked questions that made her feel seen: "Are your parents proud of you?", "How long is an overnight shift, really, it seems very long?", "Does the damp get into your bones down there?" When Carmen came along, they all went dancing.

At home, Maria put Pinkerton's gifts—tinned peaches, chewing gum—on the pantry shelf. Her mother eyed them, suspicious of what he might ask in return; her father pretended not to notice and, later, cut the peaches into exact quarters so each of Maria's brothers got the same.

"Do you like him?" Carmen asked one afternoon over a chipped mug of tea in the Bonnici kitchen. The kettle wheezed; the window fogged; outside, a neighbour shouted at a chicken.

Maria considered. "He is...alive," she said, searching. "Like a match. He makes a lot of light all at once."

"And then?" Carmen's eyes were kind, but unblinking.

"Sometimes matches last long enough to light the stove," Maria said, and they both laughed.

One night in late April, Maria came off shift early to find only Charlie waiting by the bastion gate. He shifted, uncomfortable.

"Where is he? Has something happened to him?" she asked.

Charlie's mouth tightened. "No, he's fine, but he's gone to Strait Street."

Maria knew what that meant. Strait Street was notorious, a place of bars and dancing girls, of liquor and laughter and scandal. Her heart tightened.

Maria looked past him to the slice of harbour between roofs. "I see."

"I told him not to," Charlie said.

"You are not his father," Maria said, and wished she had not. The hurt on Charlie's face was quick and honest. "I'm sorry."

He shook his head. "You deserve better," he said, very quietly. She said nothing, only nodded and walked home alone that night.

Maria slept badly. In the morning, she told herself she would end it—whatever *it* was. That evening, Pinkerton waited under the same lamp with the same grin for a heartbeat; then the grin faltered.

"I'm sorry," he said without preamble. "I was blowing off steam. It won't happen again."

Maria wanted to believe him.

"Do you say such things to every girl?" Maria asked, more curious than angry.

He shook his head. "I don't say things like that to girls. I say them to you."

"Words are cheap," Carmen said from the shadows; she had paused halfway down the steps, arms crossed.

"I know," Pinkerton said, looking at Maria, not at Carmen.

Maria held his gaze for a long moment. "We will see," she said.

At the next dance, Carmen came determined to dislike him and failed in the first half hour. Pinkerton did not drink more than one weak beer; he did not show off beyond what the music permitted; he did not press his luck. He made Carmen laugh and thanked Charlie when he wordlessly took his place fetching water and paper cones of roasted chickpeas.

During a slower tune, Pinkerton and Maria moved carefully together. "I thought," he said, eyes on the floorboards, "that the only way to be seen was to be loud. Then I met you."

"You are still loud," she said, but her voice was soft. "Just—less."

"That's Charlie," he said. "He's like ballast."

"Ballast?"

"Keeps a ship from tipping over."

"Then thank you, Mr Mason," Maria said when the song ended, and Charlie, who had not been near enough to hear, blinked at being thanked and said, "You're welcome," because it seemed safer than asking why.

The wind shifted. More ships came. Lorries growled at odd hours, and men in new uniforms asked for directions to locations that had suddenly become destinations.

Pinkerton still made mistakes. He told a joke once that belonged on Strait Street and regretted it before it finished leaving his mouth; she raised an eyebrow, and he apologised as if she was his commanding officer. He reached for her hand one evening, and she pulled it back, not ready; he stepped away without sulk or show and, two nights later, asked permission and did not hold on longer than she allowed. He was learning not to be the loudest thing in the room.

"Why do you like him?" Carmen asked with genuine curiosity under the teasing. "Besides the Coca-Cola."

Maria thought. "He listens," she said at last. "Not always. But more than I expected. And when I am afraid, he makes me feel safer for a while."

Carmen nodded. "Charlie does that all the time. Quiet men are like cellars. They keep things cool."

Maria laughed. "Then perhaps the four of us make a house."

"Don't get carried away," Carmen said, but she was smiling.

On the last evening of April, low clouds flattened the sky, and the sea smelled of spoiled fish. Maria came up from the underground and found Pinkerton alone under the lamp. Charlie, he explained, had been called back to the ship for a briefing. "Which means," he added lightly, "that if I misbehave there is no one to kick me."

"Then don't misbehave," Maria said.

He fell into step beside her. "I keep thinking I should say very impressive things to you," he said after a moment, "and then I remember you like warm socks and honest maps."

"I like not being lied to," she said.

He nodded. "I can do that. I can try."

They walked in companionable silence, wind tugging at their shirts, the bastions beneath their feet, old and patient as the sea. At St. Paul's, Maria paused.

"Will you wait?" she asked. "Just for one candle."

"I'll be here," he said, and stood bareheaded by the door while she went inside.

Her prayer was brief and inelegant. *Show me his true face. And if it is not for me, make me brave enough to see it.*

When she stepped back into the chill, Pinkerton was where she had left him.

He did not ask what she had prayed for. He only offered his arm for the walk home, and when she took it, the searchlights above the harbour swung lazily on, uninterested in two small figures tracing a line of stone toward a future that, for tonight at least, did not have to be decided.

Love and War

S ummer crept toward Malta with sticky heat and restless nights. The harbour bustled, with convoys coming and going, and rumours spreading like flies. Maria heard them in the plotting rooms; Carmen heard them in the bread queues.

The weeks that followed were full of heat and dust. The days slowly grew longer as April turned into May and summer. The days became warm and damp, the air heavy with salt. The island felt restless, bristling with rumours. More ships in the Grand Harbour, more lorries rumbling along the streets, more soldiers in crisp uniforms asking directions in accents from half the nations of the world. Everyone felt something was coming.

The air felt softer now, with fewer sirens warning of air raids, fewer bombs falling. The air smelled of orange blossoms and sea spray. Valletta, though battered, with piles of rubble everywhere, was returning to life: shopkeepers painting shutters, church bells ringing even more loudly, children daring to play in the streets again.

"Another convoy's due," Carmen said one evening as she and Maria climbed the steps from the War Rooms. "You'll be busy tomorrow."

Maria nodded. "Always busier before something big."

Carmen grinned sideways. "He'll be waiting again. You know he will."

"He waits when it suits him," Maria said, but there was colour in her cheeks.

Pinkerton still waited for Maria most evenings. Sometimes Carmen joined them, sometimes she didn't, but when she did, she teased Maria mercilessly. "You blush too easily," she said as they walked together one evening. "If he smiles at you in the dance hall, half of Floriana will know how you feel before the first tune ends."

Maria shot her a look. "You are worse than my brothers."

"Your brothers don't see you mooning over him when he's not there."

"I do not moon."

Carmen laughed and twirled once on the road. "You moon. But I like him better now. He's trying."

Pinkerton was always a whirlwind of energy and talk, spinning stories about baseball games he used to play, his hometown Chicago, about anything but the war itself. Charlie said little but watched them with quiet eyes, and Maria was grateful for his presence. He made her feel safer.

The island was buzzing — convoys coming in at night, lorries trundling from Valletta by day, fresh troops disembarking at the harbour. Everyone whispered that something big was coming. Some said Sicily; others said Greece. Maria knew better than to ask questions, but she felt the tension tightening like a spring under the city streets.

Pinkerton grew more restless, his grin a little sharper, his jokes a little louder.

"It's going to be soon," he told her one evening as they walked past St. John's Co-Cathedral and listened to the bells striking curfew. "When it happens, it'll be fast, and we'll be gone before you know it."

Maria nodded, her stomach fluttering. Each time he mentioned leaving, she felt the ground tilt under her feet. He brought gifts—chewing gum, canned peaches, chocolate bars. She knew she shouldn't accept, but it was hard to say no when her little brothers at home stared with wide eyes at the sweets she brought back.

At the next dance, Pinkerton brought Charlie and a friend from the ship who played trumpet. The hall was crowded, windows fogging with breath. Charlie danced once with Carmen, then retreated to the side of the room. After a while, he and Maria sat together while Pinkerton fetched drinks. Charlie glanced toward the band and said, "He does like you, you know."

Maria looked down at her hands. "He likes everyone."

Pinkerton was a whirlwind—never still, always laughing, always ready with a joke or a story. Sometimes Maria caught Charlie's eye over Pinkerton's shoulder and saw the faintest shadow of worry there. Charlie was a different sort of man, steady and soft-spoken. He walked Maria home on the nights Pinkerton was on duty. He never said much, but once, as they stood in the narrow street outside her house, he said quietly, "You're a good girl. Don't let him hurt you."

Maria didn't know what to say. She nodded and went inside, but the words stayed with her.

A few days later, after her shift, Maria found only Charlie waiting. "He's gone down to Strait Street again," he said, grimacing.

Maria sighed. "Then I will walk home alone."

Charlie hesitated, then said quietly, "He doesn't think. He's not a bad man, but he doesn't think past tomorrow. Be careful, Miss Bonnici."

Maria nodded once and went home without another word.

One Saturday evening in late June, Pinkerton appeared at her door with a determined look and a bottle of real Coca-Cola, cold from an ice chest on his ship.

"Big dance in Floriana tonight," he said. "You have to come. Might be our last one before I get shipped out. You can't say no."

"Shipped out?" Maria's heart thumped. "You're leaving?"

"Soon. Orders are coming through any day now. It's the big show—we've been planning it for months." He lowered his voice. "Sicily first, then maybe Naples. The whole show's about to start. Don't tell anyone."

"And after?" Maria asked.

"After?" He shrugged. "Another port, another convoy." He grinned at her. "Don't look like that. I'll come back here."

"You cannot promise that."

"Sure I can," he said lightly. "And I can promise I'll think about you in every port. That's better than nothing."

Her stomach fluttered. This was it, then. The rumours were true. She nodded.

The dance hall in Floriana was full to bursting that night. The band played louder and faster than usual, and everyone danced as though to banish fear. Pinkerton spun her until she was breathless, until the music and the war and the world blurred together. Swing music bounced off the walls, drowning out the faint thud of distant artillery. American sailors twirled Maltese girls, British soldiers stomped out clumsy jitterbugs, and the air smelled of sweat, beer, and perfume, Maria's shyness was swept away. For a moment, the war melted away.

Afterward they sat outside, the night air cooler than the steaming dance hall. The moon was bright. Pinkerton lit a cigarette and offered her one. She shook her head.

"You never do anything bad," he teased.

"I go out dancing with an American sailor," she said. "My mother thinks that is bad enough."

He grinned. "Then I guess I'd better make it worth your while." He leaned closer, and she felt her heart race. His lips brushed hers—light, quick, gone before she could think.

"Ben!" she gasped, scandalised.

"Relax, Farfetta." His grin softened, "I'm not going to bite."

But he kissed her again, and this time she didn't pull away.

The next week passed in a blur. Maria worked her shifts, saw Pinkerton when they both were free, and found herself thinking about him even when she was meant to be concentrating on the logbook. She noticed the way his hair curled when he came off duty, the shape of his hands as he smoked a cigarette. She had never felt like this before—giddy, weightless, terrified.

Her mother noticed the change and frowned. "You are too distracted. People will talk," she warned. But her father only chuckled. "Let the girl have some happiness," he said. "This war has taken enough."

Carmen came with them one night and caught Maria smiling up at Pinkerton as he mimed batting a ball. "Careful, Farfetta," Carmen whispered. "He's halfway to catching you already."

Maria elbowed her, but she was smiling too.

Orders came through one blistering afternoon. The harbour below was alive with movement, silhouettes of ships shifting into position. Pinkerton met her outside the War Rooms, his face shining with excitement.

"It's on," he said. "We sail tomorrow night."

Maria's stomach dropped. "So soon?"

"War waits for no man." He grinned. "Or woman. But listen—come with me tonight. We'll go dancing one last time. We'll make a night of it."

Maria hesitated. She wanted to say no, but she saw the hope in his face and nodded.

That night, the hall was even more crowded. The band played loud and fast, and Pinkerton seemed determined to burn the night away before morning. They danced until Maria was dizzy, until her feet ached, until she could hardly breathe. When the music finally stopped, he led her outside into the cool night.

"Come on," he said, taking her hand. "Let's walk."

They wandered through the sleeping city, past shuttered shops, and empty piazzas. The moon was high over the bastions, silvering the harbour. Pinkerton stopped at the Upper Barrakka Garden.

"I wish I didn't have to go," he said softly. He turned to her. "I don't want to leave without telling you," he said softly, "when I get back, I'm going to marry you. Make it official. Then no one can scold you for walking with me."

Maria's breath caught. "Marry?"

"Sure. You're the only good thing about this place. When this blasted war is over, we'll find a priest and do it right. You're the prettiest girl I've ever met. I want to make sure you'll be here when I come back."

Her heart beat wildly. She had dreamed of this, but to hear it aloud was something else. She hesitated, "but we are not married yet."

He smiled, coaxing, stepping closer. "Then let tonight be our promise. Give me something to fight for. Make me believe I'll come back. Soon as I get back, I'll find a priest and do it properly. But tonight—tonight we can seal the deal."

She frowned. "Seal the deal?"

He stepped closer. "You love me, don't you?"

She nodded, unable to speak.

"Then trust me. It'll make me fight harder out there, knowing you're really mine. That you're waiting."

Maria heart hammered, torn between fear and longing. Everything in her upbringing told her this was wrong, but he was leaving, and tomorrow he could be gone forever and the thought of losing him forever was worse. She was seventeen, in love, and the war could end everything tomorrow. The war could snatch him away like it had so many others.

"All right," she whispered.

Later, Maria lay awake in the small room he had borrowed from a fellow naval officer, listening to the hum of mosquitoes beyond the netting. Pinkerton slept beside her, one arm thrown carelessly across his chest, already snoring. She felt shy, exposed, a little ashamed—but also strangely proud. Whatever happened next, she belonged to him now, in a way no one could take from her. Tomorrow he would sail for Sicily, and she would wait.

Betrayal

T he following night the convoy sailed from Valletta, engines growling like distant thunder. The harbour was alive with the sound of engines, the tang of diesel, the shouts of sailors. Maria stood on the bastions among the other women, waving until her arm ached as the flotilla slid out to sea, one vessel after the other, their wakes shining silver in the last rays of the setting sun. Somewhere out there Pinkerton was leaning on the rail, grinning at her, she told herself. He had promised he would return.

When the last ship was a smudge on the horizon, she went to church, *St. Paul's Shipwreck,* and lit a candle. She knelt, whispering prayers into the cool hush of the nave. *Please keep him safe. Please let him come back to me.*

It became a ritual. Every evening after her shift, she stopped at the church, lit a candle, and prayed for Pinkerton's safe return. Even on days when the air raid sirens sent the city scrambling for shelter, she prayed, even when bombs fell on the Three Cities, she prayed. Even when she heard news of ships sunk off Sicily, she prayed. The war was a monster that could swallow men whole; her prayers were the only weapon she had.

The first letter came two weeks later, short and smudged. Notes written in Pinkerton's sprawling hand, posted from Sicily. They were light, cheerful, full of jokes.

> *Dearest Farfetta,*
> *Still alive. Sicily is hot enough to fry an egg on the deck.*
> *The boys are gambling with lira we don't have and cursing in three languages.*
> *I keep telling them I've got a girl in Malta who'll have my hide if I don't come back.*
> *Thinking of you.*
> *Save me a dance. — Ben*

Maria read it until the pencil marks blurred. Carmen teased her—gently, for once—about smiling at nothing while stirring soup.

Another followed a fortnight later:

> *Farfetta,*
> *Had my first real espresso in weeks.*
> *Thought of you with every sip.*
> *If you ever see a soldier humming*
> *Glenn Miller at dawn, that's me pretending you're near. B.*

Nearly a month passed. Another note arrived:

Things are moving fast.
You'd like the stars here.
Save me a dance. B

Each letter from Pinkerton — short, jaunty, smelling faintly of ship's ink — she carried folded in her pocket until the paper grew soft with wear. Maria carried them like talismans in the pocket of her dress. But then the letters grew sporadic. A month passed.

Another month passed. Then another note arrived from Italy:

Butterfly,
You wouldn't believe Naples—chaos
and beauty and wine that tastes like church
feasts.
We sail again soon.
Keep those candles burning. — B.

After that, silence. Weeks stretched into months. Malta's summer beat down on the stone streets; the War Rooms stifled under the heat of bodies and maps. Maria kept glancing at the bastions each evening as if willing him to appear.

She tried not to worry. She tried to convince herself it was the censors, or the mail service, or the confusion of the Sicily landings. But an emptiness began to grow in her chest. Perhaps the ships were slow. Perhaps the post was delayed. But a hollow feeling grew in her chest.

Summer weighed on Malta like a wet towel, hot and humid. The plotting rooms grew stifling. The nights rang with lorries and distant guns. Maria worked, prayed, and waited. When she and Carmen climbed the bastions after shift, Maria looked out at the dark water, hoping for a miracle.

"You'll make yourself ill," Carmen warned. "He's not the only man on the island."

Maria said quietly, "He is the only one who makes me feel seen."

Carmen sighed and let it go.

One afternoon Charlie appeared at the War Rooms with a folded paper. His uniform was dusty, his face drawn. "He's been sent to Algiers," he said. "Shrapnel scratch. Nothing serious."

> *Farfetta,*
> *Don't let the word "hospital" scare you.*
> *Just a scratch. The nurse here is too bossy to let me die.*
> *The coffee is terrible, so I plan to recover out of spite.*
> *Write me something sweet*

so I have an excuse to get out of here.
Yours, B.

Maria took the letter with shaking hands. She pressed the letter to her lips when she was alone. She wrote back, pouring her heart onto the page.

Come back soon.
There is something you must know.

She tucked the letter under her pillow until she could send it.

By late August, the nausea began. She blamed the heat, the tinned meat, the long hours—until she missed her monthlies and the truth settled like a stone in her stomach. But the sickness stayed, and then her body betrayed her in other ways—her waist thickened. The truth became impossible to deny. Carmen noticed first.

"You must see a doctor," Carmen whispered one night, after walking home with her.

Maria went pale. "No. I know what it is."

Carmen's eyes softened. "Pinkerton?" Carmen's voice was very gentle.

Maria nodded, tears slipping down her cheeks. "He will come back. We will marry."

"And if he doesn't?" Carmen asked.

"Then I will still have his child."

Carmen squeezed her hand and said no more.

But the secret was harder to hide. By October, her dresses were tighter, and the women at the War Rooms began to whisper.

When Sergeant Camilleri noticed, he called her aside, looking anywhere but at her face. "You know the rules, Bonnici. You cannot stay on shift."

"I can still work."

"It isn't about work." His voice softened. "Your father will need to decide what is proper."

Proper meant shouting in the Bonnici kitchen, neighbours whispering over walls. Her mother's face hardened when she found out. Her brothers stared in open curiosity.

Her father was silent a long time before he said, "you cannot stay here and bring shame on this house. You will go to the Sisters in Gozo. They will know what to do with the likes of you."

Her mother turned her face away. "We brought you up well, and this is what you do? Have you no shame?"

Maria wept. The parish priest came and spoke kindly but firmly: Gozo would be best until the child was born. She went to her room and collected her things in a small bag.

The ferry to Gozo was crowded with soldiers and crates of supplies. Maria sat apart, her shawl pulled close around her, staring out at the blue-grey sea, watching Comino slip past. Carmen had come with her as far as the ferry dock and had pressed a parcel of fruit into her hand, hugging her hard.

"You are not alone," Carmen whispered, hugging her fiercely. "I will write. And I'll come when I can. And if he writes—tell me first," she said.

"Write me everything, and I'll write back," Maria said.

She had already written to Pinkerton; *There is something you must know. Please come back.* She sent it with the fleet mail and prayed.

The Sisters of Charity met her at the landing and took her to the convent near the cliffs, a pale building smelling of soap and sea air. They gave her a narrow bed and plain dresses and put her to work in the laundry and in the kitchen, keeping her hands busy so her mind would not unravel. There was no judgment in their faces, only quiet discipline, and daily routine. Each evening, she knelt in the little chapel. "*Keep him safe,*" she prayed. "*Let him come before the baby does.*"

No reply came.

Maria settled into the rhythm of the convent. She prayed with the sisters, scrubbed sheets, cooked meals, and tried to quiet her racing thoughts. Letters to Pinkerton went unanswered. Weeks became months. Maria worked hard, grateful for the routine, but her heart ached every time she heard the bell calling the nuns to chapel. She knelt with them and prayed harder than ever. *Keep him safe. Bring him back to me. Let him love me still.*

In February 1944, under a rain-swept sky, Maria gave birth to a boy, the sea roaring outside the convent walls. The labour was long and hard. The nuns prayed with her through the night. At dawn, a cry rang out and they placed a son in her arms. Maria wept, but the sisters were kind, and when they placed the tiny boy in her arms, she forgot the pain. He was small, dark-haired, perfect and for a moment the universe fell away. She named him Joseph, after her father, praying it might soften his heart.

She wrote to Pinkerton the next day, telling him of the baby, telling him that she was waiting for him. She posted the letter with trembling hands. Weeks passed with no reply. She wrote again, and again, her words becoming more desperate.

Carmen came when she could, bringing news from Valletta, holding the baby, making Maria laugh for a little while.

"Perhaps he has not received the letters. Perhaps the letter was lost," Carmen said gently.

"No, he must have," Maria said. "He must come back. He promised."

But at night, when the convent was silent and Joseph slept beside her, Maria cried into her pillow. Somewhere in her heart she knew.

That night she knelt longer than ever in the chapel. "*Show me his true face,*" she prayed. "*If he is not coming back, let me see clearly. Make me strong enough to do what must be done."*

The wind rattled the shutters, and Maria felt the quiet settle over her like a verdict.

Meanwhile, across the Mediterranean, Pinkerton had been fighting his war. Sicily had been taken quickly, and now the Allied armies were pushing into mainland Italy. Pinkerton's ship ran supply runs up the coast, dodging air attacks and shore batteries. One grey morning, a shell struck close aboard, flinging him against a bulkhead and leaving him with cracked ribs, few broken bones, and a concussion.

When he woke in the naval hospital in Algiers, Kate was there.

"Ben," she said softly, brushing the hair from his forehead. She wore the white uniform of a Navy nurse; her face tanned from the African sun.

He grinned weakly. "Kate. You came back to me."

She laughed, half-tearful. "I was always here. You're the one who went running off to play war."

They fell into old patterns easily. When he was well enough to walk, he took her out into the city, the narrow streets, and French cafés. One evening as they left a café near the harbour, a bomb exploded in the distance, rattling the windows and sending people running for cover. Kate clung to him, trembling.

"That was close! We could die tomorrow," she said.

Pinkerton kissed her hair. "Then let's not waste more time."

Two days later, they were married by the Navy chaplain, Charlie and Kate's friend standing silent as witnesses. Pinkerton was all smiles, Kate radiant in her simple white dress. Only Charlie seemed sombre.

Afterward, as they drank a toast with the other officers, Charlie caught Pinkerton's arm.

"You going to tell Maria?" he asked quietly.

Pinkerton's grin faltered. "I'll write. Later."

Charlie said nothing, but the look he gave Pinkerton was harder than any words.

By spring, Maria's letters were no longer hopeful but pleading. She prayed every day, lighting candles, kneeling until her knees were raw.

And still, no word.

Then one morning, standing at the chapel door, Maria saw a figure she knew. Charlie Mason stood in the courtyard, his cap in his hands. Her heart leapt—Pinkerton must have returned.

"Where is he?" she asked breathlessly.

Charlie's face told her everything before he spoke. "He's not here, Maria."

"Is he—" Her voice broke.

"No, he's alive," Charlie said quickly. "But—Maria, he's married now. To a nurse in Algiers."

The world went still. She felt as though the floor had shifted under her feet. Charlie sat her down on the cold stone bench. Maria gripped the edge of the bench until her fingers hurt.

"No," she whispered. "No!"

Charlie's face was full of regret. "He sent me. He read about the boy in your letter. He thought—he thought it might be better if the boy came with us. He and Kate can raise him in America as their own. Give him a proper home."

Maria stared at him, tears running silently down her face.

"Please think about it," Charlie said kindly. "I'll come back in a few days. You don't have to decide now." He squeezed her hand gently.

He turned away, leaving Maria standing in the courtyard, the wind from the cliffs whipping her hair.

That night she went to the chapel and knelt in the candlelight. The statues of the saints looked down impassively.

"*You were meant to keep him safe*," she whispered to the Virgin. "*You were meant to bring him back to me.*"

Her voice broke into sobs. Somewhere in the dormitory, the baby cried, and she went to him, gathering him up and holding him close.

"*I won't give you up*," she whispered fiercely. "*Not to strangers. Not to America.*" she whispered, "*If this is Your will, let him have a good life. But let him stay on this island. Let me see him sometimes.*"

But the question gnawed at her. Next day she prayed, asking for a sign. She spoke with the Mother Superior, who reminded her gently that every child deserved a home, a loving home, where he would not be a source of scandal.

The following afternoon, a couple from Rabat came to the convent — friends of the order, childless after years of hoping. The man was a clerk in the Governor's office, quiet and respectable; his wife had kind eyes and a soft voice. They spoke to Maria with gentle respect, asked to see Joseph, and when she placed the baby in their arms the woman's face lit with joy.

Maria watched them for a long moment, her heart aching. She knew her decision was made.

That evening she knelt again before the Virgin's altar. "*If this is Your will*," she said softly, "*then I will let him go. Let him grow strong, let him grow gentle, let him be loved, knowing this sea, these bells, this sky.*" She told the Mother Superior her decision.

Joseph was christened the following Sunday, the wife holding him, another couple standing as his godparents. Maria stood at the back of the chapel, tears running silently down her cheeks, but there was a kind of peace in her heart. She had given him a future, and in time she might watch him grow from a distance, even if he never called her mother.

When Charlie returned, she met him in the courtyard.

"Tell him," she said quietly, "that the boy is provided for. He need not come."

Charlie's face was a mixture of relief and guilt. "I'll tell him," he said. Then, after a pause: "I'm so sorry, Maria."

She nodded but did not answer.

The Return
Valletta July, 1945.

B y the time Pinkerton returned to Malta, the war was finally over in Europe, although it was still being fought in the east. He came ashore leaner, older, but still with that easy grin that had once melted Maria's resolve. He was no longer Lieutenant Benjamin Franklin Pinkerton, U.S. Navy. Now he was Ben Pinkerton, salesman for a machinery company out of Chicago, ex-officer turned salesman, carrying more regrets than luggage.

Malta looked very different. The siege was long over now, the streets full of noisy shoppers, merchants, and children playing again under the patched facades of bombed-out houses. Scars of bomb craters were slowly disappearing. New buildings were rapidly built to take the place of the old. There were cafés open on Strada Reale, women gossiping on balconies, and fresh paint on the shutters.

He leaned on the rail of the ship as it edged into the Grand Harbour and tried to shake off the knot of guilt that had been sitting in his chest ever since Charlie had told him.

Charlie Mason met him in a café off Merchant Street. He was greyer now; his uniform marked with a senior officer's rank. He was now stationed outside Naples. "You look different," Charlie said after they shook hands.

"Everyone looks different after a war," Pinkerton said grimly. "She gave the boy away?" he asked again, for the fifth time.

Charlie stirred his coffee, watching him. "Yes. You know she's still at the convent."

They found Carmen at the market. She looked at Pinkerton for a long moment, then said flatly, "You waited too long."

"I want to see her," Pinkerton said. "Where is she?"

"In Gozo," Carmen said. "Today she takes the veil."

"She gave her child to a family she trusts," Carmen added gently. "Now she gives herself to God."

"She can't just erase me," Pinkerton snapped. "He's my son."

Carmen's dark eyes hardened. "You had your chance to be a father. She begged you to come."

Pinkerton flinched, but Charlie touched his arm. "If you want to see her, we'd better go. You may yet catch the last bell."

Carmen shook her head. "You should have come when she wrote. She had Joseph, and she had to face it all without you."

Pinkerton cringed at the name. "Joseph."

"She named him for her father," Carmen said. "He's a good boy. Healthy. She loved him enough to let him go."

"What does that mean?"

"She gave him to a family in Gozo. A couple who cannot have children. People she trusts. She says it is better this way."

"I came to see her. She gave my son away, Charlie. I have a right—" Pinkerton said.

"Yes," Charlie said shortly. "To a respectable couple here in Malta. Good people. He'll have a proper home."

"She had no right!" Pinkerton's hands clenched on the rail. "He's my son."

Charlie's expression hardened and he turned on Pinkerton sharply. "You have no right, Ben. You made promises you never intended to keep. You forfeited that right when you left her here, pregnant, and never even bothered to write back. You left Maria to face this alone."

Pinkerton flushed. "I was fighting a war."

"And marrying Kate," Charlie said flatly.

Pinkerton opened his mouth, then shut it.

Pinkerton flushed. "I want to make it right."

"Make it right for her — or for you?" Charlie asked quietly.

Pinkerton said nothing.

"If you want to see her, we'd better go," Charlie said.

The crossing was silent. The convent stood white against the island sky, bells tolling like a heartbeat. The sea was calm, the sun bright, but Pinkerton stood at the rail with his jaw set. Charlie sat on the bench. He had agreed to come with him, though not without protest.

"Don't expect a warm welcome," Charlie warned.

Pinkerton didn't answer. His eyes were on the low cliffs ahead.

The convent was quiet when they arrived, the air heavy with the scent of sea salt and rosemary. A young novice led them to the courtyard and asked them to wait.

Pinkerton paced, his shoes loud on the flagstones. "She has to see me," he said. "She owes me that much."

"No," Charlie said quietly. "She doesn't."

Pinkerton swung on him. "You're supposed to be my friend."

"I am. And as your friend, I'm telling you that barging in here now isn't going to undo what you did."

Before Pinkerton could reply, the Mother Superior appeared. She was a tall, spare woman in a starched wimple, her face calm and unreadable.

"Lieutenant Pinkerton," she said. "We have received your request. You have come a long way."

"I want to see her," he said. "Maria."

The Mother Superior folded her hands. "Sister Maria, or Miss Bonnici as you knew her, has considered the matter. She does not wish to meet you."

Pinkerton stared at her. "She can't refuse me!"

"She can," the Mother Superior said firmly. "The boy is safe and well, raised by good people. He now has parents who love him. You will not disturb that — or her."

Pinkerton's hands curled into fists. "He was mine. She had no right—"

"You have no right," the Mother Superior cut in sharply. "You left her with nothing but a promise. And she has built a life out of what you abandoned. She bears you no ill will, but she has chosen a different path. She is preparing to take vows."

Pinkerton blinked. "She—what?"

Pinkerton felt as though someone had struck him. "She's—she's becoming a nun?"

"Yes. God has called her, and she has answered."

"That's insane," Pinkerton said, his voice rising. "She can't just shut me out like this. She has my son—"

"The boy is no longer hers," the Mother Superior said, her voice firm, with a hint of rebuke. "Nor yours. He has parents who love him and a future free of scandal. You will not disturb that."

Pinkerton's face went red. "I have a right—"

"You have no rights here. This is Malta, not America," she said. "Mr Pinkerton, go back to your own country. Leave this island in peace. She no longer is part of your world. Now go!"

Pinkerton opened his mouth to argue, but Charlie put a hand on his arm. "Ben," he said softly. "She's made her choice."

Then came the closing sound: the heavy wooden door of the cloister swinging shut, sealing Maria's choice. It was not loud, but it was final.

For a long moment Pinkerton stood there, his fists clenched, his breath coming fast. Then he turned on his heel and strode out of the courtyard, his boots loud on the stones.

The Mother Superior inclined her head to Charlie. "She will pray for him," she said quietly.

Charlie nodded and followed Pinkerton out.

Inside the convent chapel, Maria had heard every word. She was kneeling behind the grille, a small, knitted cap which she had made for Joseph clutched in her hands.

She had thought her heart would race, that she would weep to hear Pinkerton's voice again. But instead, she felt calm, as though a long storm had passed, and the air was clear. Joseph was safe; her sacrifice complete.

"*Thank you,*" she whispered to the Virgin. "*For keeping him away.*"

The bell rang for Vespers. Maria rose, crossed herself, and went to join the sisters in the choir stalls, her voice rising clear and steady in the cool evening air.

Outside, Pinkerton stood at the edge of the cliff, staring out at the grey-blue sea. "She didn't even see me," he said hoarsely.

Charlie was silent for a moment. Then he said, "It's her choice, Ben. To live a life you can't touch."

Pinkerton swore under his breath and turned back toward the road.

"I didn't mean for it to end like this."

"No one ever does," Charlie said. "But you don't get to write the ending alone."

On the ferry ride back, he stood apart, staring out over the water.

But Maria's face—young, laughing, radiant—stayed with him all the way back across the channel.

At sunset, the convent bells rang for vespers. Maria's voice rose with the others, clear and steady. Somewhere down in the village, Joseph's new parents were bringing him in from the garden. She imagined him safe, warm, growing strong under the same sky that arched over her.

And for the first time in months, she felt at peace.

Regret
Valletta, 1950

The city gleamed in the sunlight, Merchant Street bustled with shoppers, the cafés spilling tables out onto the pavement. Pinkerton walked slowly up the street, feeling the weight of memory with every step.

He was no longer a naval officer, no longer married either. Now he was just Ben Pinkerton, of Chicago, a salesman with too many ghosts.

He finally admitted to himself, that Kate had been right. She had taken one look at his wandering eye and packed her bags after three years of marriage. He had tried to laugh it off, tried to fill the void with other women, but Chicago was full of ghosts now. Ghosts with dark hair and shy smile who had never forgiven him.

He turned down toward Old Bakery Street, heading for the café where Charlie had agreed to meet him.

Charlie Mason was already there, in a crisp officer's uniform, a little greyer at the temples but otherwise unchanged. He rose and gripped Pinkerton's hand firmly.

"Ben."

"Charlie."

They sat. A waiter brought them coffee, thick and sweet. For a moment they said nothing, listening to people chattering in multiple languages around them, the sound of church bells marking the hour.

"You look better than the last time I saw you," Charlie said at last.

Pinkerton huffed a laugh. "Better on the outside, maybe. Inside? I'm not sure." He stirred his coffee, staring down into the dark liquid. "I thought I'd come back. I just need to see her. One last time."

Charlie's expression didn't change, but he nodded. "You know where she is."

Pinkerton nodded. "The convent."

"Yes. As you know, she took her vows. She's Sister Maria now."

Pinkerton swallowed hard. "Does she ever—does she know I'm here?"

"She will, if you go," Charlie said.

They drank their coffee in silence. Finally, Pinkerton set down his cup and stood.

"Will you come with me?"

Charlie hesitated, then nodded.

They took the ferry to Gozo the following morning. The sea glittered, calm and blue, Pinkerton stood silent at the rail. Gozo was green when they arrived, the fields bright with wildflowers. The convent looked much the same as Pinkerton remembered — whitewashed walls, quiet.

The Mother Superior met them in the courtyard. She had aged, but her eyes were still keen.

"You have come back," she said.

Pinkerton nodded. "I only wanted to see her. From a distance."

The Mother Superior regarded him for a long moment, then said, "She knows you are here. She will pass through the chapel on her way to Vespers. That is all she will permit."

"You may wait in the chapel."

Pinkerton's throat was dry as he entered the cool, dim chapel, filled with the scent of wax and rosemary. He sat in the back pew, with his hat in his hands. staring at the altar, listening to the faint sound of the sea outside. Charlie stood at the door, hands clasped behind his back.

The bells rang. Footsteps approached. The sisters filed in, one by one, their white veils glowing in the candlelight.

And then she was there.

Maria — Sister Maria now — walked with the others, her head bowed. Her face was calm, serene, untouched by the turmoil that had once consumed her. She passed within a few feet of Pinkerton, and though she never looked up, he felt the air shift, as though she knew he was there.

He sat frozen as the sisters took their places and began to sing, their voices rising like a tide. The sound was heartbreakingly beautiful, filling the chapel with something that hurt and healed at once.

Pinkerton bowed his head, suddenly and unexpectedly ashamed. She had chosen this life, and he had no claim on her, no claim on the peace she had found.

When the singing ended and the sisters filed out, he remained seated until the last echo faded.

"Ben?" Charlie's voice was gentle. "We should go."

Pinkerton stood. His face was wet, and he wiped it quickly with the back of his hand. He followed Charlie out into the courtyard.

"She didn't even look at me," he said hoarsely.

"Maybe that's her mercy," Charlie said.

Pinkerton nodded once, staring back toward the chapel door. "She's free of me now.".

They left in silence. As the ferry carried them back to Malta, the sun was setting, turning the sea gold. Pinkerton stood at the rail, watching the island recede. Somewhere behind those white walls, Sister Maria was praying for someone — perhaps even for him.

Epilogue – the Last Butterfly

Sliema, 1984.

The kitchen is quiet when Joseph closed the diary. The last page still smells faintly of lavender, as though Maria herself had been there moments ago. He sits for a long time, staring at the closed book, his fingers resting on the worn leather.

His wife comes in softly. "You've been reading since breakfast."

"She told me everything," Joseph says, voice thick. "All these years, and now I finally understand why the butterflies were delivered."

That afternoon he drives to Gozo with his eight-year-old son. The convent lays white against the sun, much as Maria had described it. In the small cemetery behind the chapel, he finds her grave: a simple stone with her religious name and the date of her death carved deep.

Joseph kneels and places a single lace butterfly on the grave. The wind lifts it for a moment before settling it gently back.

"Thank you," he whispers, "for the life you gave me."

His son crouches beside him, small hand resting on the stone. "Was she brave, Papa?"

Joseph's throat tightens. "Braver than anyone I've ever known."

The convent bells ring for vespers, echoing over the fields. Joseph stands, taking his son's hand, and turns toward the sea. *Another year, another butterfly,* he thinks. The last butterfly trembles in the breeze, catching the light as if Maria had given her final blessing.

THE END

Author's Note

I t all began at Teatru Manoel in Valletta in 2023, when
we attended a performance of *Tosca*. It was superb. I
have always loved Puccini's *Tosca* — not only for its soar-
ing music, but for its perfect fusion of love, politics, and
tragedy. Teatru Manoel staged the classic version, set in
Rome in 1800, with its Napoleonic intrigues and courtly
maneuverings.

That evening set me thinking: what if Tosca's story un-
folded in a more recent time, when the stakes were just as
high? Malta in the summer of 1941 — bombed, starved,
and ruled by curfew — seemed the perfect setting for
Bastion of Shadows. Valletta's bastions, churches, and
theatres offered a stage already inscribed with courage, betrayal, and sacrifice.

The result is a Tosca who walks through blackout
streets, sings to a city under siege, and fights for love in a
world we can almost still touch. It remains Tosca's story —
but it is also Malta's: a tale of love, courage, betrayal, and
defiance on the edge of the bastions, where stone meets sea
and the night breaks into a terrible dawn.

Thinking of Puccini brought me to another of his operas, *Turandot*. The music is magnificent, but the libretto has always struck me as deeply flawed: set in a mythical China that never existed, with a "love story" built on riddles and cruelty, and a princess who changes her mind because of a kiss. It never made sense to me.

So, I moved the story entirely and wrote **The Bastion Protocol**. This *Turandot* is not set in some imagined Peking, but in present-day Valletta — a real fortress city at the crossroads of Europe, Africa, and the Mediterranean. Turandot is no longer a vengeful princess but a brilliant cybersecurity architect, guardian of a system that could make or break Malta's sovereignty. Calaf is not a love-struck prince but an ex-intelligence officer striving to avert a geopolitical disaster. Liu is his former MI6 colleague, now a whistleblower whose sacrifice truly matters. Puccini gave us drama and music; I wanted to give the story stakes that felt worthy of them — riddles that demand more than clever answers, and a heroine whose final choice could topple a government.

The final story, **Bastion Butterfly**, reimagines Puccini's *Madama Butterfly*. While the opera's music is exquisite, its libretto is troubling and ill-suited to modern times: a fifteen-year-old girl from a poor family in old Japan, married in name only to an American naval officer, abandoned with heartbreak and a child. That story ends in despair.

Instead, I wanted to imagine what might happen if Butterfly had more choices — and a chance to live beyond sorrow. Setting this tale in wartime Malta allowed me to explore love, faith, and resilience under curfew. Maria's journey is my tribute to Puccini's opera, and my way of giving Butterfly her own ending. It is still a story of young love — but it is also Malta's story: of love, courage, and betrayal on the edge of the bastions, where stone meets sea.

Acknowledgements

A special thanks to my editor, Cathy Eberle in UK, and also my cover designers at GetCovers.com located in Lviv, Ukraine.

And to my husband, Alan, who took me to the opera. Over the years we've seen everything from Carmen to Madama Butterfly, from Don Giovanni to Tosca. From Turandot to Lucia di Lammermoor.

A.K. Lakelett

December 2025

PS. Thank you for reading my books. I hope you liked them.

If you have a moment, please leave a review on Amazon or GoodReads. And thank you!

More from the author

If you'd like to check out my other books, those are old fashioned whodunit's set in Faukon Abbey, Devon, England.

Book 1 – Remember Me? What happens when your past catches up with you? A chilling mystery that will haunt you long after you finish reading it. A man is found dead with no identification, not even a mobile phone. Who was he? Who saw him dying in Tersel Woods, near a small town of Faukon Abbey in Devon, England?

Book 2 – Missing Alibi Was it something she wrote? That's the question investigators, DI Greene, DC Ford, and their journalist friend Carter are asking, when a popular author of mysteries, and romance is found dead after a party. Were her new stories based on facts rather than fiction? Did the stories she had written, make someone angry enough to kill? The lengths people go to keep their secrets hidden...

Book 3 – Death of a Well-Travelled Man When is a death a murder? There's trouble brewing in the idyllic town of Faukon Abbey. The main employer, Gwedrow Glassworks plans big layoffs and tempers flare. When Marion Rivers, a pillar of the community, is found lifeless in her bathtub, DI Peter Greene gets suspicious. A cyclist disappears; another one is injured. As secrets emerge, yet another chilling death further shatters the peace.

You can find out more about Faukon Abbey and my books on my website

www.aklakelett.com

You can also sign up there to be a member of my readers group and get a free book and a booklet about Faukon Abbey for free!